Wade Parrish

Winchester, UK
Washington, USA

JOHN HUNT PUBLISHING

First published by Zero Books, 2021
Zero Books is an imprint of John Hunt Publishing Ltd., No. 3 East St., Alresford,
Hampshire SO24 9EE, UK
office@jhpbooks.com
www.johnhuntpublishing.com
www.zero-books.net

For distributor details and how to order please visit the 'Ordering' section on our website.

Text copyright: Wade Parrish 2020

ISBN: 978 1 78904 820 9
978 1 78904 821 6 (ebook)
Library of Congress Control Number: 2020951522

A CIP catalogue record for this book is available from the British Library.

Design: Stuart Davies

UK: Printed and bound by CPI Group (UK) Ltd, Croydon, CR0 4YY
Printed in North America by CPI GPS partners

We operate a distinctive and ethical publishing philosophy in
all areas of our business, from our global network of authors to
production and worldwide distribution.

For William

Illustrations by Jack

1.

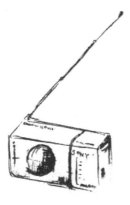

Today is Tuesday.

It is always either Sunday or Tuesday in —— and it is usually either nighttime or late afternoon. Always in Daylight Savings Time. Always at the very changing of the seasons.

In the late afternoons on Tuesdays, Susa comes on WQQX and plays the obscure back-catalogs of small known Estonian jazz singers. The jazz singers have thin and winnowed voices and sound very far away in their recordings. Like postcards deposited into sewer grates. Or grocery lists muttered through in dreams.

I ride the H11 bus on Tuesdays and listen to Susa through the headphones of an old gray SanDisk audio player. The ear cushions on the headphones are peeling. The people on the H11 have yellow eyes and haven't seen a face for 18 hours. Beaten to silt. The bus smashes over potholes. Very few people have use for their pupils in —— and most only see the world through an ooze of white sclera. Like their irises have been chipped off or smudged away or painted over with detailing paint. And their whites have all grown yellow from the glare of old bank machines and staring far away for far too long. I have the feeling now like there's someplace I ought to be, but it is not the place I'm going. Susa is partial to a female contralto named Tuli, whose music is Post-Soviet, who slurs every 3rd pulse.

:And how can it be? There are dreams left to dream? Before we die, or waken?

Susa translates the lines his listeners call in for. A small coterie of shut-ins somewhere to the west of Lithuania-town. Where all they have left now is the radio. The bus dry-heaves (6) times before it reaches Oak Park. The wind is cold when the doors splay open. The air from the harbor is thinned by rows of empty blocks and blocks of empty rowhouses. And it should be said now that the sky in —— can make you claw your eyes out. Fingers full of silt. Every time the bus stops, I think, surely no one can live *here*. And each time, another one exits. Carrying a plastic bag. Wheeling a squeaking cart. Handling a cane or a walker. Reaching into their coat pocket for rosary beads or a prescription bottle or a rope of japamalas. Surely, no one can live *here*, I think, just before Oak Park shoots up.

-I've been having a lot of problems tasting things recently, a woman tells her companion.

-Don't get dramatic about it, the companion replies.

Oak Park is a cluster of apartment buildings sprouting out around a depleted duck pond, a jungle gym, a circle of interlacing sidewalks. The jungle gym is roped off now by tattered streams of yellow caution tape, flapping in the wind like jaundiced fingers. No one uses the jungle gym in Oak Park anymore. The paint on the metal is toxic. It tints the palms of what it touches a municipal green. They built the jungle gym here for the children of computer plant workers, decades ago. Low-cost housing. Brick and stucco. There used to be a school here and a churchyard and a daycare center nearby. All since gone. I get off the bus.

:Don't fall away without me, love, can't you see your stain on me, broken?

Ms Tupelo stands outside the apartments now. She is smoking and tilting her head to the side. Ms Tupelo rents me my room here. It is a very small room on the 14th floor and at first, I asked her a lot of questions about the heat and the internet connection and where I'll go when I die but she just stared through me with her eyes yellow and softly blinked. No one thinks all that much in ——. There are a lot of landlords here. Six for every tenant.

Ms Tupelo remembers when they used to make computer chips here and cries at night because they don't anymore. She says three words and then coughs for half an hour. She plants Virginia Slims in the potting soil of blue succulents and lights them all like incense sticks. Sometimes I email her about the drip in the shower or the black mold beneath the sink and she sends me back old still photographs from grainy documentaries about Warsaw and Tallinn with foreign expletives in the subject line.

-Sad day today, she tells me as I'm passing.

-Mm.

Ms Tupelo starts to cough. I wait until her coughing breakers into hacking, stemming up black blood onto the flat of cracked pavement. Her face purples. The old wrinkles on her neck shake and the spindle hairs on her skull shake and eventually she waves me on. Ms Tupelo is a frail woman with dark and venetian features. She wears black shawls in the winter and black shawls in the rain. She has a thin nose and skin like yellow eyeballs and a way of being like a leaf, saying maybe she'll rot away somehow. Or like the figure of a woman alone in the painting of a minor Dutch master. She's been sick for a long time now but refuses to check into St Killian's. Now she leans against a rusted handrail as the sky above us darkens, casting shadows on the walls. There are no more bikes parked in the bike rack at Oak Park. Only a single rusted wheel someone has left shackled to the absent aluminum frame.

I turned Susa off in case Ms Tupelo had something more important to say and now that he's off, I forget he was on to begin with. I pass beneath the brick façade of Oak Park where the fire escapes curl upwards into the spines of separate and broken kitchens. I call the elevator, pushing the yellowed button and listen to the sound of gears mashing as the box makes its ascent. It is a poor thing to trust one's life with, an elevator. But we do. And when the elevator arrives, the box is empty except for Mr Kim. He has ridden up from the garage in the basement.

-How are you today, Mr Kim?

-Hrmph, he says.

There are just two people in ——.

There are people like Mr Kim and Ms Tupelo who have lived here forever, and there are people like me who have lived for about six months. These two clans resent one another with something like a virus. They mistrust one other. They can only see each other for their flaws and there are many flaws. There are too many flaws to get into now, but slowly they will push their way up through the soil like a burning pack of Virginia Slims.

Maybe it is wrong to say people live in ——. No one truly lives here. People exist in —— and for different periods of time, but it's not a place anyone truly seems to live.

Susa can't reach me through the elevator walls, even when I turn him back on. He is describing the winter of 89 again. His voice hums a slur of crinkled static. Mr Kim pulls out a tangled nest of dental floss from the pocket of his bathrobe and begins running the wire through gaps in his teeth. The elevator smells of cinnamon and kimchi half-digested. His teeth are like old rusted Galloway stones and soon the lights in his skull will be flipped off one by one. His gums begin bleeding. The elevator halts at (14). I get off.

-Goodbye, Mr Kim.

-Hrmph.

The walls of my corridor are tilting.

All of the doorways down the yellow hall are green chipped doors with tainted gold eyelets and tainted gold numbering. I have the need to knock on my own door but don't. The key has to be jammed into the lock several times before the bolt can open.

My room is small and empty. Earlier I began collecting road signs to hang from the walls but now they all slouch unguarded, with some in stacks and others in piles. I don't like the signs with words on them very much. All my road signs are just arrows without letters and most of the arrows are bending away from each other. I don't remember where they all came from anymore. Flat slats of iridescent metal I've collected showing orange. Red. Yellow. Green.

All my furniture belongs to people who have long since left —— and left behind their couches and chairs and ugly white armoires. The kitchen is wet and connects to the bedroom in a fluid stretch of warped hardwood. I sleep in a hammock these days. Like an organ in a sack or like blood in an organ. It makes the floor seem very empty and clean.

My walls are yellow. They look like eyes. Like elevator buttons.

The main room yields to a smaller bathroom with the drip in the shower and the black mold beneath the sink. The drain in the bathtub is broken. It is always in the process of draining. I'm afraid the drain is slowly shrinking the bedroom and wetting the kitchen with its sink. I stuff yellowed paper into the black hole of the drain when I want to take a bath and it works alright for a short while. The ink from the print has stained the bathtub basin to the point where every chemical will not clean it. I don't even remember when the bathtub was clean.

I stuff the drain with paper from an old phonebook and twist the hot handle as far as it will go and turn Susa back on through a flashlight radio I keep hanging by a hook beside the toilet. Tuli sings with the clatter of the filling tub. Taking off clothes now has been like taking off just one coat or an extra sweater or an excess scarf or shawl in the shrinking space of the cramped bathroom. It has been this way since I first moved to ——. I have been permanently dressed for about six months. My skin will not peel.

When the water is tall enough to sink into, I climb inside. Tuli's song is almost over. Her song is almost over when she begins to skip beats. First every other beat, then every two. Then every four. And then eight. And then silence. She repeats the dying lines as they linger off into silence and into bathwater. Like the strings of yarn they used to hold on the decks of departing vessels traveling far away. There is no rush to finish things in ——.

:*I long for you, my one my true, for now lay strangers in my oceans.*

For you, my One my True, I think, the bathwater circling my chin.

I don't like it when Susa forces rhyme to his meanings. I don't know who calls in for this, but their wants are very particular. It is not the Lithuanians, it must be someone else. The tiles around the bathtub are cracked with broken brown lines and the wallpaper is made of rusted floral patterns. My cell phone rings from a limp pocket on the tile. I can see the blue-glow lighting up through the pocket. The plastic shaking violently on the floor. Like an old rheumatic landlady. I reach over the bathtub edge and open it with wet fingers. Lil is calling.

-Hello, Lil.

-Hello. Did you enjoy the song?

-Yes, but I only caught the very tail end of it.

-I don't like it when Susa uses metric translation.

-I don't think anyone does.

-Why does he do it then?

I don't say anything and sit back in the tub. The water sloshes audibly around my shoulders and gurgles above the drain. The water is not hot.

-How is your bath? Lil asks.

-It's ok.

-Is the water warm?

-Not particularly.

Lil sighs. Susa believes silence is palate cleansing. He waits the full length of the oncoming song before the oncoming song is played. He breathes into the microphone as he waits, and I hear him breathing through the flashlight and Lil breathing through the phone and then Susa breathing again through Lil's radio where it plays on the other side of the line.

-What are you doing tonight? she asks.

-Just taking a bath.

-And after that?

-Getting out of the bath.

-And after that?

-I don't know, I tell her absently. I've been feeling sort of blue lately. Maybe going over Jersey.

-No you're not, Lil says suddenly. Don't say that. Don't talk like that tonight.

-Ok you're right. I'm not.

-Good. Will you come over then?

-If you're asking.

-Then I'm asking.

-Then I will.

Lil hangs up. Susa is still breathing. The drip from the shower falls between my shins where the ink curls up from the drain like twisted black fire escapes around an invisible building. No one talks on the phone for very long in ——. Few have cause to talk at all in —— and fewer still have the need to talk with anything as warm as a voice. Many people have forgotten their own languages from going so long unspoken to. Lil talks on the phone still but only because she hasn't been really living here for very long. About six months. I close the phone and slide it back toward the pocket.

When Tuli begins to sing again, I sit up and claw the paper out from the drain. I hold the paper pulp in my hands without looking and fling it into the toilet. The drain gurgles and sucks away more of the room. A great deal of paper gets caught in the drain and has to be unclumped from time to time.

2.

I call for the elevator and catch Mr Kim on his way down from roof level. He clips his toenails now, leaned unevenly against the elevator siding like a swan crumpled along its spinal cord. The nails eject in high white arches away from where his ankle rests upturned against his knee.

-Alright, Mr Kim?

-Hrmph.

The elevator drops. Mr Kim's toenails curl around his toes and he needs to wedge the clippers beneath the curl and cut the curl before cutting again. The numbers above the sliding door count backward to (7) where Lil lives. Lil and I have shared the same building since she arrived in ——. Lil doesn't like the building very much. She thinks Ms Tupelo will be dying soon and doesn't know what happens when a landlady dies without an heir and without a will.

-Maybe we get to keep our rooms, I told her.

-Don't be stupid, she said.

The elevator stops at (7). Mr Kim lowers his curled foot and gives me two dead-pupils and a stern handshake.

-Goodnight, Mr Kim.

-Hrmph.

An identical floor spreads forward and I hook in the direction of Lil's room. The doors on (7) are all chipped blue with rotting silver numbers and rotting silver eyelets. I find Lil's room and fondle the handle but the lock holds still. I knock.

-Just a minute, Lil calls.

It is usually just a minute with Lil. She needs time to polish the corners of her bedroom for dead skin and pick the spent fabrics up off the floor. It is not something she does particularly quickly. There are tiny rubber weights attached to her blood vessels. Tiny sacks of mass looped around her platelets that keep her from moving very fast. She loses extra hours this way, effectively condensing her days. She tries on the same outfit five times in the mirror. She fixes her hair.

-Thank you for waiting, Lil says finally, opening the door.

-It's no problem, I say.

Lil nods. She's wearing a bath robe with her hair tied up under a towel. Her face looks like she's been washing it with rubbing alcohol for several days.

-Thank you for coming, she says gently.

-It's no problem at all, I say.

She turns back inside. Lil's room is bigger than mine, but she pays less rent for it. It is not uncommon in —— to pay less rent for larger rooms. There is a certain luxury to less space here.

-Something to drink? Lil asks.

-Do you have any apricot juice?

-I meant with alcohol.

-Apple then?

-You're hopeless, Y.

-Very true, I say.

Lil collapses into the big iron-cloth sofa and sighs. She drinks red wine from an old carafe. She sighs loudly enough to echo, and I look away.

The most defining feature of Lil's sitting room is the oversized, waist-high drumkit standing across from the sofa. The drums are not rock drums, but a kind of double-wide neon bongo set with a melodica hewn into the wood. The melodica mic curls up like a broken finger. The drums are very loud in all ways and take up half the room. Their neon sidings are not electric but glow anyways in strips of red and blue and green down the frontside of the drums. Like traffic signs without arrows on them. Lil only plays when there are people around. I am not exactly people so she probably won't play. Besides the drums, the room is orange and the walls feel very thick.

-I broke up with Sam today, Lil tells me.

-Yeah?

-I wouldn't say it if it weren't true. Do you think I'd lie for fun?

-I didn't say 'yeah' because I thought it wasn't true. I said 'yeah' because I thought you might go on about it.

Lil frowns. Her bathrobe is lemon-yellow and there's a black towel tied around her forehead. The towel curls up like a flattened snake, three shades off from the shadow of her skin. She crosses her arms.

-Are you surprised?

-Not really, no.

-You're not surprised?

-No.

-Even after the engagement?

-Especially after the engagement.

Lil frowns again. Her lips are thin and ruddy and beneath their curtains, I'm sure her pearl teeth are wine bled and drooping. The relationship was a very mediocre thing. Lil is capable of very mediocre things.

-You don't believe in me at all, Y.

-It's hard to believe in people, I say.

-Is it because of Lucy?

-No.

-Is it because of Jacob?

-No.

-Is it because of Ruby?

-No.

-Then what is it? she asks. Am I a pattern to you? Like hound's-tooth or tartan?

-Like Chinoiseries, I tell her. She glowers.

-No one ever knows what the hell you're even talking about when you talk, Y.

I suppose Lil is right. I sit down on the sofa a good ways away and she flinches. She places the carafe on the floor and adjusts her head towel and doesn't look at me directly. She is waiting on a question. Something to circle down the fractals of her mind like wet slips of paper down a bathtub drain. Lil has a hard time loving anything or anyone very fully or for very long, but she likes to run the string out on things as long as the other person is hanging on. Something happened to her a long time ago to make her this way but isn't that the story of everyone. I feel bad for Sam as an engaging charade, but not much as an actual person. There are a lot worse ways to get to —— than to fall miserably in love with Lil.

-Do you feel bad about it? I ask.

-Awful, she says. Sam was very sweet. It's terrible when awful things happen to sweet people. More so than when they happen to the rest of us.

She pours the carafe down her throat and I watch as her esophagus pulses. Her face is very dark in the gloom light of the sitting room. I think of tiny fishes swimming in the base of the carafe. I think of the tiny fishes they use to clean the callouses off people's feet and wonder if they would develop fish to clean out the callouses in one's insides. Tiny fish swimming through bile ducts, intestinal streams and chakra channels.

-It's not so awful, I say to Lil. It can always be worse.

-Can it?

-Absolutely.

-Well I suppose that's a good thing then, she sighs.

Lil stands up from the sofa, swaying, and walks away back into the back rooms of her overlarge apartment. I sit alone with the neon bongo set and the faded campaign posters that cling to the soft orange walls. I think Lil used to be into politics, maybe. Months ago. She used to say things at meetings. She used to bang her palms against a podium board and point with her index fingers. I listen to the sounds now of fabrics rustling in the back room and hear Susa playing again, low and sober through the doorway. Lil hums sometimes and she is humming now, along with a jazz singer who is not Tuli.

Lil re-enters the room in a white satin pajama slip and her hair sprung out. Lil has short neon peroxide hair that beacons in a crowd. In better lights, I have said the peroxide is for Lil like an old spinster lighthouse keeper, shining its spotlight out to avoid the mulish conclusion of ships in the night. A gesture of desperation.

-Well? she asks.

-Is it lighter?

-No, darker, she tells me. My roots have been threating recently. I'll need to dye it again soon.

-I see.

Lil nods.

-Did you hear the one about Orion's belt?

-I didn't.

-It's a big Waist of Space.

-I see.

Lil frowns again and slides back onto the iron-cloth couch and takes a heavy swig from her carafe. Some of the wine leaks from the edges and runs down the corner of her mouth. It gives the impression of a rotting fruit. Like the acceleration of a still-life painting. When the apricots and apples all turn to mush.

-You never smile, Y. All the time I see you, you never smile.

-It hurts my face to.

-Does it?

-Yes, I tell her. I have a plaster face and if I smile, it might all crack up.

-You're very annoying, Y. Did you know that?

-Well.

Lil touches the neckline of her slip. In the evenings, we used to sit together and memorize the names of small islands in cloudy Polynesian chains. We used to freeze strings of yarn into ice cubes and wear them as necklaces until our shirts were wet and our collarbones were shivering. Anything to break the time.

And when she's with someone, I would fade up into the 14th for a little while. Do jigsaw puzzles on top of road signs. Try memorizing sections of the phonebook. Lay in my hammock for days and wash my face in the sink and take long baths and think of all the things I would do differently again if I could. Lil and I have never really tried to be with one another, but I think we tolerate each other quite a lot sometimes or need to tolerate each other if we can. She knows we can't, but still she waits around like harbor birds when in the interim of another abortive love. Lil thinks her clavicles would make great mallets for the drums. Mine too, she thinks.

-Did you see that mystic yet?

-No.

-Y, you promised.

-I know I did.

-Don't you want to?

-Want is a funny word.

-It might be nice if we could.

-For who?

-You don't think it would be nice?

I sigh. Lil continues to knead her clavicles.

-Why don't you play the drums? I ask.

-I'm too tired.

-Just for a little bit. You never play the drums for me.

Lil shakes her head. She eyes the drumkit warily. She picks the carafe back up, now half-drained and keeps drinking. When she was with Sam, I would sit on my fire escape in the cold and listen to the drums four floors below pouring out into the night with the bleary whine of melodica weaving in between the thumps. She played slower for Sam than she did for Ruby and slower for Ruby than she did for Jacob and for Lucy she hardly played at all, but only tapped the edges so soft I could hardly hear them. This is when I first moved to —— and thought the tapping was a silver bug that had gotten trapped beneath the floorboards. It would keep me up at night.

-How do we know what's ethical anyways? Lil asks me.

-Don't start.

-I'm only just saying.

-You always only just say.

-But have you thought about it?

-Of course I've thought about it. Why wouldn't I have thought about it?

-So you admit it might be nice then?

-With you?

-Who else?

-There are other people, I say. Lil laughs dully.

-For a person who doesn't smile, you sure make some pretty good jokes.

Poor Lil. That's all I can think. Poor Lil. I stare at her head and the white glow and wonder if when she sees me, does she think: 'Poor Y'? And I think she probably does. I am not good company anymore. Perhaps I never was. But there is a lot of bad company one will endure in —— so as not to be alone. Maybe why Lil plays the drums so much. To chase out the ghosts. She tips the carafe. She wipes her mouth and sucks her legs up tight beneath her body. She swills the red remaining third in the fishless glass container.

-Did you hear El went over Jersey?

-No, I say. When?

-Day or so back.

-That's really terrible.

-It is. I feel bad for Ng.

-They were close?

-Very.

-It's a shame.

-Truly.

-Maybe it's contagious.

-Maybe.

I think back to what I said in the bathtub and feel bad now. I should tell Lil I feel bad but I don't. Lil rubs her forehead and runs her hands through the thicket of white where it shoots up close above her. She is sad for El and sad for Sam and sad for life in general. Sometimes before from the mouths of other people, I've heard it said that Lil is a whole host of horrible things, but she is not. Not really. To say so would be to buy the common misconception that people are the ways they are because that's how they choose to be. Lil is her desperation just as I am. Just as we all are. Uncontrollably passive things.

-What are you thinking? Lil asks.

-I was just thinking about how we are all our desperations.

-What the hell does that mean? What desperation?

-There are a lot of desperations, I guess. Desperation is wanting without knowing what you want. Or wanting what doesn't exit. Or can't exist. Or won't.

-And you think I'm desperate?

-Especially.

Lil furrows her brow. The room is still and orange and quiet.

-You shouldn't tell people what they are, Y, she says.

-Because I'm wrong?

-Because you'll always be wrong when you try to tell people what they are. They won't believe you. People always think they're experts on the subject of themselves.

-I guess so.

-And you never know all the facts.

-I guess so.

Lil is right. Lil is usually right when I try to say things bigger than the room and the day and the weather. The rim of her mouth kneads at its corners and her eyebrows fold.

-It's hopeless, Lil sighs at last. I don't know why I called you down here, Y. You're so horrible for cheering someone up. You're always looking for things to be wrong about. You're always saying those awful things.

-I'm sorry, Lil. Should I be something else tonight?

-If you could.

-I'll try then.

-Likely.

I stand up from the sofa in the main room and go into Lil's bedroom in the back. The walls inside are plastered black and white with photographs of her and Sam smiling by the reservoir and at the aquarium. She makes faces and sticks out her tongue when the camera flash goes off in her palm and the fish behind her tap their noses on the glass. Sam looks at her with open eyes that suck Lil's face inside them with love. There are odd lover's objects still scattered in the room that make no sense outside of a dead lover's language, hanging from bookshelves, pinned to cork board, littering the dresser top. Totems. I have seen these photographs before with different faces. There will be big black trash bags filled with memories soon.

Love doesn't go anywhere when it dies. Maybe that's why I'm so uncomfortable being down here. Many times in ——, there is only a thin film or shell surrounding what's truly painful. Vacuoles of memory waiting to burst. Lil is so much more courageous about it than I am. She is pretty courageous about that kind of thing. Or reckless. But it's painful to be in proximity either way.

After Lucy, I rode with Lil out to the docks and flung the trash bags into the harbor. They floated in the water with the other trash and became indistinguishable. Lil was very sad that day. I thought someone might try and stop us. A policeman or someone from the City. No one did. Soon the walls will sprout new photographs of a different person that will all smile in the exact same way with the exact same set of eyes and faces. Lovers always feel the need to spread their disease like that. Diseases always feel the need to replicate themselves over again, using the plans of new bodies to repeat the same patterns on their skin.

It should be noted now that a cat does not drown in a trash bag because the trash bag sinks. A cat drowns in a trash bag because it begins to claw, letting in the water through tiny claw-sized holes in the bag.

I pick Lil's radio up from on top of her bed, from the tangled and tearstained bedsheets. Her radio is a silver box with speakers on either side of a cassette mouth. I lift it from the yellow sheets and the gentle bleed of fairy lights and bring it back into the hall. I don't like seeing the bed where Lil has laid crying and tangled beneath dead photographs for so long. It is not a place that makes much sense to me. Why she would go back and rehash it.

I flick Susa back on and its silent static and breathing. Lil tilts her head around as I drape the radio onto the sofa. The carafe is all gone. It is a small glass body. Lil is too tired to sit anymore and so she rises like a trash bag in the harbor, bobbing and sways into the bend of my arm.

-Are we dancing now? she asks me.

-No, I say. Not yet.

Her head sticks to my collarbone as we wait through Susa's breathing. Her face is hot with wine that has not yet boiled over into tears. My hand makes a shelf for her fingers in the air as she places her palm on the small of my back.

-Thank you, she says.

-It's no problem.

The music drifts on with radio crackle. It's Tuli again. Her voice is thick and violet and I move Lil in a slow sweep over the floor. She fits clumsily in my arms like a used conjunction, leading off to another dependent clause, half-submerged down a bathtub drain.

The past tides through Lil's body in an unrelenting ache as we dance. I don't remember in ——, or I try not remembering in ——, but now the wavering shadow of what was seems to seethe through Lil's shoulder blades as we dance because

2

Lil remembers too much and it's all infectious. All of what's before floats, trapped in plastic, like cats in trash bags along the surface of my brain. One of Lil's many diseases. I remember red tears in abandoned shopping centers on the tired parking lots of the gray Southeast. I remember losing people, people I loved, I think, maybe, sometime ago. I remember patiently staring out of melting windows, waiting for the day to arrive and having arrived, to end. I remember leaving and never knowing how to leave, and always having left, or being in the anticipation of leaving, and when the leaving came, looking to leave again. That is the way it is in ——. And none of the dead loves or dead lives make sense to the living, like Aramaic or the languages that ghosts speak. It's easy to tire of repeating the names of past lovers to current lovers on the tired pile of tear-dry bedsheets, as Lil does. But she does it. There is always more than one reason to move to ——.

Lil's feet cut across mine unevenly and eventually I pull her up to stand on my shoes and sway her like a curl of smoke. Her clavicles are likely made of glass, I think.

-Can't we be murderers? she whispers into my chest. Just this one time?

-It's a very bad habit, I tell her. And probably a hard one to break.

She nods. She smells like a pollen in a sewer grate. The nature of the curse is hard to imagine and harder still to explain and there are many who doubt that it's true. I don't ever doubt that it's true because I see them at night, circling around the hammock and asking questions in languages I don't understand.

Sex is also very lonely in ——.

Outside, a siren wails. The siren wraps up several floors of tenement loft to remind us now how there is someone always dying here. The police in —— typically exist to call the paramedics and the firemen work more to contain than to save.

Tuli's voice cuts the siren as it comes into the room off-time.

Worse than off-time. Tuli seems to hear the siren and make space in the beat for its wedge as we sway. —— serves a reminder to itself of itself in the wail of service vehicles. Anyone who stares at the ceiling in the darkness long enough will know the different pulse of emergency vehicles and be able to tell apart their choruses in the night. This is an ambulance siren. Tuli trails off.

:*I am half a heart without you, love. I am half-asleep while dreaming.*

Susa maybe could have said 'your loving' to force the rhyme but he doesn't. Maybe it means something. That there is no pattern in these suggestions. Old runes carved into a crumbling wall. I was so absorbed in the siren and in Tuli that I hadn't noticed Lil had started to cry.

-She sings a lot about dreaming, doesn't she? Lil says softly.

-Wouldn't you?

-I don't know, she wipes her nose on my shirt. I don't know what I'd sing about. What would you sing about, Y? If you could sing?

It's not the kind of question I really like to answer but it's very hard to refuse crying people. I rest my lips on the top of Lil's head but leave them limp and kissless.

-I'd probably sing about desperation.

-You would, wouldn't you.

-Yes, I probably would.

-It's probably good you don't sing then.

-Yes, it probably is.

Susa's hour is winding to a close. He ends his set by ranting about the inner dealings of the Estonian Parliament. There are names that reoccur in the rant but there is typically only the blank and vapid space of cursing that swells a little from one sentence to the next until the engineer at the studio quietly cuts him off. The sad vacant jazz cannot contain a man like Susa.

-You know Ng is at the Gymnasium tonight, Lil tells me.

-Would you like to see him?

-No, she says. Not me. But I think he should be seen.

-Would you like me to go and see him then?

Lil breaks away from me. She picks up her carafe and disappears into the back bedroom. I see her lips sideways as she brushes past me and her lips are soft now like hairs and tongues and fingers. The door to her bedroom slides to a crack. I listen to the sound of clicks as she lights her candles. The engineer turns the volume on Susa's microphone progressively lower as his rant grows progressively louder. The words in Estonian gradually weigh down the English until the English is only stones in dark water, sinking into the sea of syllables curling up around them. All the anger and the energy is still in the tone but the lid is being closed slowly on Susa. The close of the program makes me think. Whatever will be, will be. Whatever will be probably is, in a seed somewhere. If I will be dead, I have been dead already. I turn for the door.

-If you're coming back tonight, Y, please bring back wine for me.

-Sure, Lil.

I tell her, then leave the room.

3.

The light in the hallway has darkened even without windows. When Susa's time is up, the JV football team at —— Central broadcasts its scrimmages on WQQX. The broadcaster is an old woman with a shallow voice named Mildred. Mildred sits in the battered press box with failing vision and watches the players squirm from a pair of cracked binoculars. Her narrations are very sad, but also very poetic.

I press the call button and catch Mr Kim on his way up from the ground floor. He sits in a lotus pose on the elevator tile with a rock of pumice in his hand, rubbing the scales of his feet away. The skin particles drift like sawdust into a small clump on the floor.

-How is it, Mr Kim?

-Hrmph.

Mildred describes the wind patterns drifting in from the harbor. R. Sykes, the kicker, is prone to squib kicks and like all the —— Central kickers, he has been poached from the soccer team. Mildred thinks the wind will work against the kickoff tonight. It will blow down heavy on the ball and make the short kick even shorter. Mr Kim's pumice sounds a little like brushes on a drum kit, scrubbing away at his calloused foot.

By the time I reach the ground floor, —— Central has already lost the coin toss. R. Sykes will not have to kick. The elevator door slides open.

-See you around, Mr Kim

-Everyone I ever loved died alone in the arms of tragedy, he says.

-Ok, Mr Kim, I say.

The wind outside has picked up brighter than it was when I came home. The moon is waxing gibbous as it always is in —— and the dark sky is purple and violet and sick. Ms Tupelo is shaving her legs outside and smoking. The smoke curls up invisibly around the dark air as Ms Tupelo exhales and runs a razor down her thigh.

-Cold night tonight.

-Mm.

Ms Tupelo breaks over, coughing. Her spittle smacks the pavement in thin slivers. Her spittle is black and red like blood and mulch, like soil in a black lung or blood in a flowerpot. She waves me on. Her cigarette falls to the pavement unextinguished and her razor draws a trickle of soil. No one bothers extinguishing their cigarettes in ——. Sometimes they throw them lit into trashcans or onto nearby porches. It can be a problem sometimes.

I make for the bus stop as M. Marian receives the kickoff like a flour baby and makes a fatal stand at the 32-yard line. All the front blockers fail him at once. He falls beneath the crunch of rival helmets. —— Central begin their drive from deep in their own territory.

The cars in the lanes by the bus stop are black and white and gray. The people in the cars have more white in their eyes than the people who ride the busses but not by much. These cars were not made in ——. No one really knows where these cars were made.

There's an old woman shriveled in a black trench coat sitting alone on top of a bus stop ad selling renter's insurance. Her hair is drained into sick clumps like sticks of black kindling. J. Wyse fumbles his first snap, but —— Central recovers.

-Going somewhere? the woman croaks.

-Strange question to ask someone at a bus stop.

-No it isn't, she says. Not here.

-You're right, I say. It isn't.

I wish I had cigarettes. I think about going back to Ms Tupelo or maybe asking the bus stop lady, but I won't. I only want something to do with my hands which is not just waiting, as waiting can sometimes eat one alive. I think people probably talk about smoking a lot more or a lot less than they should for how important it can be for staying healthy.

-I can read your aura, the bus stop lady tells me.

-Yeah?

-Yeah. Give me your palm and I can do it.

She rises from her bench.

I used to carry a pocketknife before I moved to ———. If I still had it, I could peel off the skin and seal it between plastic layers of film to pass to every palm reader I ever met at a bus stop. Or I could cut off both palms and toss them into the harbor with the trash. Then I'd show the muscle and exposed bones to every bus stop Palimistrist, proving I have no palms and thus no fortune.

Now I show her my palms.

-Curious, she says, stroking the creases. Very Curious.

I pull one headphone off my ear to be polite as T. Collins makes a 6-yard gain off an inside run. Mildred says the opposing team's pass defense far outstrips Central's ability to throw over the top and running it up the gut with a hurry-up offense seems to be the right strategy and the only option.

:How often the right strategy is also the only option for Central.

The Palimistrist stares at me. Her forehead wrinkles like sobbed-through bedsheets. Her eyebrows writhe like hips in concern.

-What the hell did you do? she asks.

-Did I do?

-You know. You know what it is. What did you do?

-That's not very 'fortune,' is it? Isn't a fortune supposed to be what happens to you?

-Cut the shit, she tells me. This is all mucky. You have a disgusting palm. What was it?

-Disgusting, I repeat, letting the word linger. I see.

The bus face peeks over traffic further down the thoroughfare. The woman is still holding my palm and tracing retraced lines with the little nail on her ring finger. Central's fullback R. Miller claws to a 1st down.

-Did you kill someone? She asks. Did you kill a lot of people?

-If I did, wouldn't I be in prison?

-Only 6% of murderers go to prison, she says. Sometimes even less.

-That seems made-up.

-It isn't.

-The bus is almost here, I point out.

-Yes, she says. Will you sit with me? I want to keep talking.

I nod. I thought she was angry because of my palms, but I think she may have just been confused. It doesn't bother me that she's crazy. It doesn't bother me that she stinks like leper flesh and trash water from the inner bay. It is just nice that she would talk to me. Our bus arrives and the brakes shriek and the frame rattles as we climb onboard.

All the bus drivers in —— keep a small white statue of a black cat on their dashboard to ward off car wrecks. They never talk. Their faces are shaped like paper bags that someone might have kept a tuna sandwich in. It's hard to say. The Palimistrist and I slip our bus tokens into the broken machine and make for two open seats in the rear carriage.

-Would you like to sit by the window? I ask her.

-Oh no, would you?

-No, but I will.

I sit by the window. Now I can see the flicker of business lights and the dull sad faces of the sad cashiers. —— has been voted the city with the saddest cashiers the last (6) years running. I don't know who votes for these kind of things. —— Central punts on 4th down. The punt is very weak. The opposing drive will begin at the fifty.

-Have you been living here long? I ask the Palimistrist.

-Yes. Please don't ask me any questions about myself. I still want to know what it is you did.

-I haven't done anything.

-That's a lie. You're lying to me.

She seizes my hand. Her fingernails curl oddly around her fingertips like they're afraid to jut out. She points with her middle finger to a thick divergent crease in the right center of my palm.

-Oh that, I say. That's a scar. I used to handle barbed wire on a cattle farm in Wyoming.

She scrutinizes the white crevice. Mildred says the opposing team is partial to slot receivers, placing a lot of weight on Central's shallow secondary. The linebackers and the strong safety.

-You've been cursed, she says softly.

-To some degree, yes.

-It's a very good one.

-Mm.

-I don't mean 'good' in that it's well done, I mean good in that it seems unique. Curses can sometimes be sort of boring. Or formulaic.

-I haven't met anyone with this one, no.

The Palimistrist nods. The Gymnasium isn't so many stops from here but it's not exactly close. I wonder if I will get to see Ng compete. I forget what name he goes by now. They go by different names at the Gymnasium. For professional reasons. I should have asked Lil, but I didn't.

The opposing team makes a breakaway run for a touchdown. It happens all at once and slurs Mildred's account into a chipped blur. The —— Central secondary collapses like a black lung, like a stack of teeth all smashed together. The secondary should not have collapsed. The secondary is usually pretty strong.

:*If their weaknesses can beat our strengths, it's going to be a very long night for Central.*

-It was bad, wasn't it?

-What was bad?

-What you did, the Palimistrist presses. What you did to whoever gave you that curse.

-It's complicated.

-It always seems to be.

-This time it really is.

-Sure.

The storefronts continue to flicker outside the bus window. Sometimes there are clumps of people standing outside. They wear dark clothes and look at the bus and think about getting on soon. The bus. The tenement buildings. The bus. The tenement hulls. The opposing team scores the extra point and —— Central prepares for another kickoff. M. Marian is not back to receive this time. He's standing beside the water cooler, hoping his father is not in the crowd. There is no cattle farm in Wyoming. There will not be one for M. Marian either. There will be long walks and long drives and long sleepless nights alone but there will be no cattle farm in Wyoming for anyone.

At the next stop, the Palimistrist stands up and gets off the bus. I think I probably disappointed her but there was no way for the situation not to end in disappointment. If she were a better mystic, she might have been able to uncover the curse and its origins and a great deal many other sacred, secret things, but she wasn't. —— is full of half-mystics, half-frustrated in their partial sight. There used to be a whole house of them on one of the lower streets, something like 40 mystics all in this big Victorian mansion. There was a fire. Someone flicked a lit cigarette onto their porch and the frayed welcome mat went up in flames. The fire department worked to contain and at least half the mystics died from smoke inhalation. Out of the other half living, half went mad from being haunted by the spirits of the other half-dead mystics and of the remaining quarter, half went over Jersey for reasons unrelated to the flames. A lot of ——'s current mystics now claim to be the remaining (5) and rub ash on their foreheads and burn themselves with Madonna candles.

The Palimistrist was not one of these.

The kickoff results in a touchback.

The bus pulls to a stop at the Gymnasium front as the 1st Quarter draws to a close.

4.

Peanut works the door to the Gymnasium on Tuesday nights. He leans on a three-legged bar stool and drinks non-alcoholic beer from green glass bottles. His head shines in the light of a double-wide exit sign hanging above the Gymnasium door. The people who frequent the Gymnasium claim Peanut keeps a homemade single-barrel shotgun stuck down his pant leg and that if he ever tried to fire it, he'd blow his arm off in the process.

-Do you know if Ng has fought yet? I ask him.

-Who?

-I don't know what name he goes by. His real name is Ng.

-Well it wouldn't help you very much if you did. I don't know what goes on in there at all. I'm just the doorman.

-Oh.

Peanut shrugs. I pay the cover fee with shriveled bills and walk inside.

The Gymnasium is loud with people. Four sets of bleachers form a square circle around a chain-link cage where men step in and beat each other unconscious and sometimes dead. The bookies skulk in the darkness behind the bleachers muttering into headsets and don't watch the men at all. It's too loud now to hear Mildred's voice, so I take my headphones off.

I don't quite go up in the stands but loiter with the huddle of heads around the ringside, just enough to catch the faces of the men engaged from out of the darkness. Neither is Ng. The fight is at some point of low climax where one of the promoters has managed to slip a green painted folding chair into the cage. One man with skull-white skin lifts the chair and uses it to brain the other man. It makes a sound like a dinner bell with wet paper tied around the clapper. The other man's teeth fly out in a stack. The pale man hesitates now beneath the spotlight and the blood, having only half-expected the chair to make contact.

29

He looks out into the darkness of the crowd, into the still of perfect silence. He looks like a child that has fallen off a swing set into the woodchips, waiting to see if it would make sense to cry. Without him and his chair, the crowd fails to exist. Without the crowd.

Well.

Maybe still in quiet rooms somewhere, there are men beating men unconscious and to death. There are stacks of teeth developing on paper carpets between paper walls. But it is unclear. It's not a source of redemption. It is not something they even want to do, but still something tells them to. The brained man with the shattered teeth twitches on the floor of the cage. It smells like wet copper, but I know at the Gymnasium they sometimes keep humidifiers full of diluted pigs' blood in the corners to create that smell. The smell of human leakage. Lighting the corded rope of adrenaline in the silent crowd.

I turn away and walk down to the double doors with the iron push bars that lead out from the darkened gymnasium. Away from the spotlight and the gray heads of the mob. I have to shove myself through a host of bodies but no one seems to mind. Out through the sludge of torso and shoulder blades. The bankrupt bettors, re-issuing one another's IOUs in an incest orgy of diminishing returns. Musical chairs playing out in silence, racing headlong to the bottom. I push open the doors and leave the gymnasium behind.

The hallway behind the door is white from overhead fluorescent and white tiles that reflect the light and the white concrete that absorbs it. Something in the hallway is like dying or being born. That overwhelming white people talk about sometimes. Going or not going into the light. I wonder if they made the hall this way on purpose. A programmatic touch. The door to the locker room is brown and unguarded. I go inside.

There is moaning inside the locker room. Someone is moaning in what sounds like a shower. There are rows of red lockers that have all been fist-dented and marked by the scrawl of black spray-paint and key scratches. Not in any names but just with paint scribbles, black scrawl running the length of the metal like twisted iron fire escapes. There are backless benches between the lockers as I pace down the rows. The light in the locker room feels dirty or delayed. Like the electricity is not shooting through the wires, but oozing. Leaking. Crawling limply into the gas trapped inside the lights before igniting into a cooled, unsteady flame.

On one bench, a man sits with his back turned. His skin is tan and his hair hangs down over his face in long black shards. The grooves of his spine heave with his breathing. I come up close beside him.

-Hello, Ng.

-Don't stand in my light.

-Where should I stand then?

-Don't stand. Sit.

I sit down against the lockers. Ng is slumped with his legs straddling the bench, his arms pressed against the insides of his knees. His skin glistens with wiped sweat.

-Did you see me fight? he asks.

-No, I just got here.

-Oh.

I can see around Ng's shoulders now and see his arms are bandaged like they've been attacked. His hands have been scoured into whiteness and tremble between his legs.

-Are you hurt? I ask him.

Ng doesn't respond. His face hides beneath his curtain of hair and can't be talked to. The moaning in the shower melts into the sound of running water and the buzzing of the lights.

-They threw a bike chain inside the ring, he mumbles. There were two or three good licks before I was on top of him.

-And then?

-And then I thumbed his eye sockets out.

-Did that work?

Ng shrugs. I have never seen Ng fight. I don't come to the Gymnasium often unless someone brings me. There is always a thick hoping in the crowd for a blanket feeling of life. As someone dies a little in the cage, their living siphons off into the crowd like a gust of wind blowing in from the harbor. They inhale the vapor like paint fumes in a bag. The eyes Ng took tonight must have somehow passed into the vapor but the vapor is collectively absorbed and weakened all at once, but a little bit of blood is typically worth a lot to those who are bleeding. The moaning continues in the shower.

-Do you know the score? Ng asks.

-Central was down 7 at the end of the 1st quarter.

-Ich, Ng sighs.

-Mildred thinks Central's receivers won't be a factor tonight. Their pass coverage is too strong for us.

-Hurry-up offense?

-That's what she says.

Ng rises from the bench and turns to the lockers. None of the lockers have locks on them. The fighters don't have much worth stealing. Sometimes they make shrines inside the lockers with incense sticks and backlit portraits of flat deities. When the fighters die, their shrines live on behind the iron locker grates and many of the lockers have gods left behind in them. Ng has a picture of a god with many palms and so probably many fortunes being unfurled at once. Ng flips on his radio beneath the portrait.

-What brought you here tonight, Y? Ng asks.

-I saw Lil tonight, I tell him. She told me El went over Jersey.

-He did?

-You didn't know?

Ng shakes his head. He drops his hands inside the locker. Mildred is explaining summary and predictions as the —— marching band tortures in the audible periphery.

-That's too bad, Ng says.

-Weren't you close?

-No. I was close to Rick though. I was in the other room when he went over a few months back.

-How did he go?

Ng lights an incense stick with a match and weaves the dancing smoke against the portrait. He sticks the burning rod into a holder and turns around again.

-He ran headfirst into a concrete wall.

-Neck or skull? I ask.

-Skull. His brain hemorrhaged.

-Huh. You don't get that very much.

Ng shrugs. His face is very blank.

-You get it some.

Mildred suggests Central has had some success with slot receivers. The first-string fullback, N. Adams, is currently being tested for a concussion by the —— Central trainer. Coach Palmer might have to change his strategy in the second half.

:The only option when losing is to change strategy. Sometimes only to lose some more, but in a different fashion.

-Did you know Cee? Ng asks.

-Maybe. I don't know.

-She went over Jersey too, he says. Tied her neck to a big white balloon and strung herself up.

-It must have been a pretty big balloon.

-It was. She was very small though. People saw her floating until she passed through the clouds.

-Did you see her?

Ng shakes his head. The moaning from the shower seems to tweak the edges of his eyelids. Mildred falls silent for a turn and cedes transmission to the static and the —— Central brass section. The oboes screech and wail. Trembling mouths filled with metal braces suckling chewed-through reeds. Ng turns her off without hearing the score.

-I suppose I should check on him again, Ng sighs.

He plucks the incense stick from his shrine and seals the locker shut. I follow him up the row of lockers in the trailing wisps of incense smoke that twist like white ink in black water. Ng rounds the corner and realizes how he's still holding the stick in his hand and so tosses it burning into a nearby trash bag slouched against the concrete wall. We go into the showers.

The man moaning in the shower lays beneath the streaming faucet with a white menstrual pad taped over each eye socket. They look to be freshly applied, without socket blood, but the shower water has made them loose and pulpy. The man is dressed in dark shorts and his chest is bare and his head is bald. Ng kicks the man's leg. The moaning stops like a wine cork or a hiccup. Ng turns off the shower. The drip makes the room feel very silent and bare.

-Get an arm, Ng tells me.

Together, we lift the man in his wetness up from the wetness of the shower floor. His skin is loose and clammy and like a wad of silt that might slip suddenly and unexpectedly from its musculature. I don't feel the wetness really through the thickness of my clothing because I hardly feel anything there anyway. The water on the floor begins to sink through the tiling as we lead him out of the showers. There are other Gymnasiums trapped beneath the floor and above the ceilings and behind the walls. Tiny, tired boiler rooms where sweat-faced men are betting on fights between endangered animals. Paying for sex with corpses. Trading their children in for hits of obscure homemade narcotics. Committing rituals out of the way of the light. The buildings in —— are infernal and crammed with newly inventive miseries. New perversions thrown wet onto the collective miseries of the world and collecting their enrichment, believing somehow this is a way to survive.

-Hold him steady here for a second, Ng says, transferring the man's weight fully onto me. He then disappears down the aisle of lockers as the man's chin drops to his chest. I falter and lock my bones to keep the body vertical.

-I used to be a tennis player, the blindman mumbles in my ear. I was at the Olympic trials.

-Ng was in the minor leagues for a while, I tell him. He played shortstop.

-Who?

-The man who blinded you.

-Oh.

Ng returns with two thick robes. He guides the blindman's arms into one sleeve, then drapes the robe around his shoulders and lets the blindman fumble his other arm into the hole. The man stands on his own now.

-Do you have any shoes for me? he asks.

Ng nods, then realizes the man cannot see him nodding.

-Yes, he says. I'll get them.

Ng disappears again. The blindman straightens the folds of his robe around his neck and leans against the wall.

-Why did you quit tennis? I ask him.

He touches the pads of his fingers lightly to the pads over his eyes.

-My heart wasn't in it anymore, he says.

I nod. Ng returns with a pair of rubber sandals and drops them onto the floor beside the blindman's feet. The blindman feels with his toes for the sandal flaps and slides his feet beneath them. Ng has put his robe on and curled the sleeves up to his elbows so that the bandages are still visible along his forearms. He takes the blindman's hand in his as we shuffle slowly to the back of the locker room where a back exit leads out to a gate and the gate leads out into the street again.

The Gymnasium used to be part of a middle school and the rest of the campus stretches backward from the back exit. We turn very quickly for the gate after the exit and for the street and don't see for very long the rows of tents and people set up in crowds within the courtyard. Some of the fighters sleep in those tents. Sometimes people come to sleep with the fighters or talk to them about other things. I don't know where Ng sleeps, but I don't think it's here. In the courtyard, from the light of barrel fires, one can see inside some of the empty classrooms. Words written in chalk against the darkness that can't be made out. Poltergeists still skulking the halls.

We lead the blindman back around the block toward the Gymnasium entrance where Peanut is still slouched on his stool. He doesn't see us coming until we are right up beside him and he flinches. I watch to see if his hand drops readily to his pantleg but it doesn't. He sees the robes and settles into his seat again.

-Alright then, Peanut sighs. He reaches lazily into his pocket and withdraws a plastic cell phone. He dials a familiar number. When the other side connects, Peanut hangs up.

-Alright, Ng replies.

We all four stand there on the sidewalk. The blindman tilts his head up toward the blind stars that are all white menstrual pads taped over bleeding eyes in the sky. Ng crosses his arms to display where the bike chain bit him.

-Is Central winning? the blindman asks.

-I don't think so, I tell him. It seems like they were down at the half.

A two-door conversion van pulls up to the curb in front of us and slides open its bay door. A man who looks identical to Peanut crouches in the van with his arms outstretched. He looks like Peanut's twin except with slightly darker eyebrows and a scar running along his nose. Ng leads the blindman up into the van.

-Will there be hand lotion there? the blind man asks suddenly.

-Sure, says the man with the scarred nose. The blind man settles himself into a bucket seat they've set up for him against the side of the van.

-Good, the blind man nods. My skin has started peeling.

The man with the scarred nose who looks like Peanut closes the doors. We watch as they pull off into the night away from the Gymnasium again.

-Where are they taking him? I ask.

-I don't know, Peanut says. Maybe to train.

-To train?

-To train. A blind fighter can be very effective. Or maybe to a train. I don't know.

I turn to Ng to see if this is true. He shrugs. The wind swipes the tails of his robe away. There is a pale outline on Ng's sternum from a necklace he used to wear. The necklace was a hand grenade from the Gulf War. There were a lot of questions someone might ask Ng about the necklace. Where did he get it and did it work and why did he stop wearing it. I don't know. We watch the taillights on the van shine off down the roadway like a pair of bleeding stars without their menstrual pads.

-That's really too bad about El, Ng says.

-Yes, I say.

-Was Lil close to him?

-I don't think so. Not really.

-I think Tess and El were close, Ng says softly.

-Were they?

-I think so.

I nod. Ng slouches against the brick of the Gymnasium and sighs. Peanut sits back on his stool and sighs. I bring out my Scandisk and slip one headphone over my ear to try and listen to the 3rd quarter at low volume, so low that Ng can still speak if he wants to and I'd still hear it. Central is on the 15-yard line, driving to score on 2nd down.

Tess stays with Bell in a nice loft overlooking the harbor up town. Lil and Tess spent four days together in a hot haze of what was then late autumn and I remember the drums were loud then but had no rhythm. Then Tess was with Ng and was really with Ng and for what seemed like a long time. Now it all makes sense. M. Tanner scrapes a 4-yard gain to clinch a first down for Central.

-Have you fucked Lil, Y?

-No.

-Is it because of the curse?

-I suppose so.

-Does she believe in that shit?

-I don't know if she does. I do.

-Mm.

Ng stares down at the pavement. He looks very sad now, and no doubt Tess is bleeding through his skull like a hemorrhage. His eyes slip closed. All of the beautiful, quiet lover's tones of lips and hair and fingers play in weak recordings from within him. How Sundays bloomed through their windows with their bodies drawn together, bedsheets, Tess's eyelids. All so lovely, all so equally departed and lost now forever. Lil has spread her pain in me and made me into Ng's thumbs in this moment, driven now to exact some bad blindness on a night like this. I'm not sure what kind of an errand this has become. But it cannot be overstated how much we do in —— just to keep doing.

-You don't think I'm a bad person because I've killed people, do you? Ng asks suddenly.

-No, not really.

-But you won't kill people. With the curse. Or at least you wouldn't.

-That's different.

-Why? How?

-These people probably don't expect to die, I say. They go about their days, most days. They buy their groceries. They say their prayers. They clean the lint from the drying machine before the next person uses it. The people in that cage probably expect to die. They're a little already dead when they step in. They get what they signed up for.

-Do you think I'm a little dead already then too? Ng asks.

I look away. I don't need to answer. J. Wyse sprints from the pocket and is stopped at the 3-yard line. The time left in the 3rd Quarter is quickly draining. Ng leans off from the Gymnasium wall.

-I'm going to the train, Ng says. Will you walk with me?

-Sure.

We start walking. Ng stares blankly at the black pavement. Tess had a studio full of drawings of Ng's body tensed in various poses that all drowned together in the harbor, their ink floating up with the tide. The god with many hands and the incense sticks have not always been the permanent fixture on the stand in Ng's locker. M. Tanner is stopped for a one-yard gain at the 2-yard line.

-You know one day it'll be me, you know? Ng says.

-Yes, probably.

-Do you know what happens to us when it is?

-No, I don't think so, I reply. I don't really think anyone really does.

Ng shakes his head, shuttering the empty pain of another setting, off where the bodies of the men pass on. I think about the twitching man, the man brained by the folding chair, the toothless man, twitching still twitching beneath the soft layers of dirt somewhere, twitching still at the bottom of the harbor, and with the current not quite strong enough to carry him out to sea. I feel him twitching like an eyelid, or a shop light that's broken but still stays on, not knowing what else to do.

-We don't actually know either, Ng says after a while. It's all a big secret. Sometimes we stand in a bar room with the body on the table and drink. Then Peanut deals with it later.

-I see.

J. Wyse fumbles the snap again. There is chaos on the one-yard line, right on the end-zone brink. The referees flock like harbor birds around the crash and the press box chair shrieks as

Mildred rises up to crane her weak eyes down onto the field. It seems so dumb that the Gymnasium killers don't know anything at all about death. You'd think they'd know more about death than the clergy. Than Palimistrists. Than Poltergeists.

-Are you going to see Tess tonight? Ng asks.

-I don't know, I say. Maybe.

There is a long, drawn out spool of silence passing between us. The City itself seems to walk. The buildings and sidewalks and cars on the corner seem to be shuffling like bugs on a mattress as we pace over them.

-Would you?

We stop. The subway entrance opens down the block like a toothless mouth. Like an open locker. Like a fire escape sinking through the street. I see Ng's eyes are watering now. Somehow the tears in his eyes remind me of a parallax, and how the space between two eyes and the space between the stars hold the same singular connection. The directory that holds the universe in place.

-I will, I tell him.

Ng nods. Central recovers the fumble. It is now 4th down. We keep walking further to the subway and I can see Ng will not join me any further. Coach Palmer will clearly go for it. If only the fullback, N. Adams, had not been concussed. The solution would be so easy then. Jam it up the middle. Mildred agrees. But there is no one he trusts to kick the field goal either. Out of options. Out of hope.

-You can take the (5) train all the way to Elm Circle, Ng says. Do you know where she lives?

-Yes, I say.

-You've been there?

-Once or twice.

-Before? Ng asks with all his sadness. I mean...before?

The tears in Ng's eyes tremble nearly to the point of breaking. Sad, for a killer. He wonders if I had ever seen the studio walls with the beauty of his body as it was before. And if I would bleed the pain of seeing the walls as they are now in the after, with his body no longer on them. Or carry the echoes of his pain long enough to appreciate the absence.

-Once before. I say. Then once after.

Ng nods. He walks away down the sidewalk without a word. M. Tanner aligns behind J. Wyse in the 'I' formation, ready to charge the defensive wall. Then the snap.

I'm never really sure how Ng and I met or how we continued to recognize each other afterwards. The people you know in —— just seem to sift into place. Like teeth on the floor of a prison. More often than not, you know no one, so it's lucky when anyone recognizes you at all.

M. Tanner is stopped for a loss at the two and a turnover on downs.

5.

Underground in the subway, the radio waves of WQQX are blocked or otherwise butchered. I won't be able to hear the 4th quarter unwind. I will have to think my own thoughts for a while. I would rather be brained with a folding chair.

The subway stops in —— are very far apart. Stepping on the train takes the passenger far away to far off blocks in the same city. It is not quite clear where the trains go when they die. I put that question to Tess once and she spoke of some great train god in the midnight sky who slurps up dead train lines like thin threads of linguini. I am less convinced. I have seen the freighters in the harbor and know the train links are loaded one by one by yellow cranes and are taken out on dark green ships and dumped together into the open ocean. This is the case for all trains, the good trains and the bad ones alike.

The (5) train is late.

The people on the platform seem to glow in the dull light. They wander up and down between the pillars, waiting for the train to arrive. Most are returning home from somewhere and feel their skin crawl with the ends of the day. Some peer over the platform edge down the gouged eye of the black tunnel where it recedes into deeper shades of darkness and think absently of jumping. I lean against the tiling on the wall.

A man in a green vest shuffles past me, shouldering a black trash bag. He no doubt has emerged from deep inside the tunnels where the bodies all twitch. The subways beneath —— are like an immense back porch, where people slink down beneath the sewers to die like cats. Their cat-bodies are all scooped out eventually by the green vest men into trash bags and hauled above ground. Once a year in April, when it is very cold and raining, —— holds a parade for the green vest men, where they wade through the streets and are watched on television. It is strange to see them packed together, making their way down the City drives. The man ascends the stairs and is gone again, leaving only an impression. The kind of face that reemerges later in dreams, whose origin is never realized.

-Excuse me, a voice beside me coughs.

-Yes?

I turn to see an urchin, a foot shorter than me, his teeth rot-green and his clothes patched together by chunks of weathered canvas. His breath is hot and he slithers his tongue over his bottom lips.

-Wondering if I could implore you for your vote, he says.

-You could, I say. What's your platform?

The man looks confused. His eyebrows droop to his eyelids. He wears a dirty hat from ——'s minor league team, the —— __ __'s.

-(5) train mostly, he says. I ride the (4) sometimes, on a good day. When it's hot.

-I meant politically.

-Oh.

The coming train chugs toward us. It blows the tunnel winds onto the platform with the smell of rotting cats. I wait with the Politician for our train link to settle and the wind and the sound to die back into silence again.

-You think we could chat a while? he asks.

-Sure.

The doors slide open like a wound and the people pour out

of the train corpse so we can take our turn. We sidle in. I sit while the Politician stands and gathers his thoughts among the train-car maggots.

It should be noted now that flies and butterflies share the same life cycle, roughly, and there is nothing less beautiful in maggots than in caterpillars and nothing more beautiful in a butterfly than a fly. Everyone in —— appreciates this. So then the people on the train car are all like caterpillars, and the train car is the immense leaf we rest on, blowing away through the tunnel. Change has no positive valence. Fly. Maggot. Butterfly. Caterpillar.

-I'm doing away with the whole mess, the Politician announces suddenly. I'm going to tear down this City, block by block and room by room. And I'm going to do away with the whole mess.

-Hear, hear, someone mumbles further down the train. The cars clink against one another like bones in arthritic fingers.

-What will the people do? I ask.

-We'll go out into the plains, he says. We will dig enormous holes together out in the flatland and bury the tenement buildings into the ground. We will scrape up the streets and cover their scars with sawdust. We will sell off everything that cannot be buried and burn off whatever cannot be sold. It's the only honest thing left to do in this world.

-Huzzah, someone whispers.

The Politician shakes softly when he speaks like a man brained by a folding chair. Like a man moved by the spirit. By mania. He gurgles like a bathtub drain and the people seem to care. He readjusts his hat and strokes his face and tries to rub his jawline away to the bone.

-What will we do with the money? I ask him. Once everything is sold?

-Everyone in —— will receive a plane ticket, he announces. We will all go off to live in different cities. We'll go off to Caracas and Montreal. We'll go off to Tehran and Osaka. We'll go off to Budapest and Mogadishu. We will go...We will go...

-Tallinn? someone asks.

-Yes.

-Warsaw? says another.

-Yes.

-Phenom Penh?

-Byzantium?

-Socotra?

-Yes. Yes. Yes! The Politician shouts. And more! And more!

When it seems his sternum will break, the people on the train look away. The shaking of his fingers is like the shaking of the trains. They branch out from his palms like the pack of crooked subway lines, ending in stubs at the tips of his fingernails. Resolution making is a popular platform in ——. As is the geographic cure.

-And once every five years, the Politician goes on, those who survive will return to this spot in the plains for an ice cream social. We will stand around and exchange photographs and speak in the pidgin tongues of the languages we've learned and are learning.

-What will we do if it rains? I ask.

-Then we will eat our ice cream in the rain, the Politician answers. We will eat it in the rain and taste the copper with the chocolate chip. It will be amazing. It will be really something else. Believe me, it will.

The Politician has been derailed, considering the melted ice cream in the salted field. He falls back into his seat and places his face into his upturned palms. Another subway platform flashes outside the window, but the train does not stop. One never knows what platforms the subway will choose to pass over. No one ever minds walking the extra blocks home.

-Where are we? a man turns to a woman.

-I think we're in rat's alley, she says. Where the dead men

lost their bones.

-You know...this is embarrassing, the man says. I should have never left my wife for you.

The Politician is resting now. He has grown exhausted. I look around the subway at the sparse crowd. The couple sit with the woman's head resting unhappily on the man's shoulder. Three young people stand holding the same silver pole and will not look at one another. An old lady wears a red smock over her winter coat. The young man she sits with makes different shapes with a grid of string stretched between his fingers.

All like different cities already, I think. They have their separate blocks and tenement harbors and harbors and lonely trains. Like Cairo and Tallinn and Warsaw and Byzantium, they stand in the subway car, unvisited. Their languages go unlearned, and one day they will all be buried, twitching in the plains. What cannot be buried is sold, what cannot be sold is burned. I am beginning to understand the Politician's platform now, but more so, the tower of Babel. The story is more than literal. We are separate languages onto one another. Our psychologies like scattered tongues, lost to one another in the crowds.

-And another thing, the Politician croaks. It is essential that —— maintains its triple-A bond rating. We can't let deficit spending outstrip our tax base, or else our rating sinks and it will all be more bad news from then on. The current administration has been playing tiddlywinks with the rainy-day fund.

He pulls out a paper sack from inside his jacket and holds it to his nose, inhaling in a sharp gust. The smell of industrial fumes trickles out from the bag's mouth as it slouches beside his crotch. The Politician's eyes roll back and his head tilts and I can see up his nose where the nostril hairs are tinged a shade of artificial silver. Another subway platform passes. Elm Park feels close.

-Where are we now? The man asks.

-The Sibyl's cave, she answers.

-I thought you said we were visiting your sister?

And now I remember I'm going to see Tess. Tess and Bell host exhibitions in their loft from time to time. The exhibitions are always half-finished and Tess comes up alongside her guests and says

-This will be much better when it's finished.

-Ah, they reply.

And they are never finished. There's nothing quite wrong with them, but they are never fully finished. The Politician takes another pull from his bag of paint and deflates again.

I don't know Bell at all. Only that she has supplanted Ng and Lil in a human chain of copulations, in a thread, in a tangle of thread spread between human palms. Cat's cradle. It is unclear what will become of her name in my memory. If it will be like some road sign, slouched off and collected in a shrinking room, with arrows pointing out to nowhere. A lot of names end up like that somehow and are lost in a pile. Places too. The subway brings itself to a stop. Everyone sitting is now standing except for the Politician, who gropes through the fumes back to his language in the subway car.

-Wait! he slurs, his hand wrapping around my wrist. Do I have your vote?

-Yes, of course. I say. You can have everything.

The Politician fishes in his pocket and pulls out a metal button. He sticks the button into my palm. We exchange nods and I leave the subway through the open doors.

Above ground, the air is stained by the harbor. Tess's loft overlooks the water and sees all the lights of the houseboats and the lighthouse and the steam chuck of freighter ships that act one day as pallbearers for all the broken subway cars. It's a shame that Tess has never seen them go out. Or claims she has never seen them. I don't know.

I think about tuning in for the dying minutes of Mildred and the game, but don't. I reach instead for the Politician's pin and pull it out beneath a streetlamp. The button is red and plain. It seems the Politician is up for re-election.

6.

Tess opens her eggshell door and holds its body to her chest. Her head peeks around its edge like a small bird in a gutter. The tops of her eyelids are painted gold and her hair is tied around her skull in braids.

-Y?

-Hello, Tess.

-The exhibition isn't till Sunday. It's not finished yet.

-I'm not here for that.

-Oh. Ok then. Why don't you come inside?

I nod and step through the doorway. Tess turns and leads me back into the loft. I think about hanging my coat on one of the hooks of the coatrack but don't. It is unclear how long I'll be staying. Or how long any of us will. The gesture casts a shadow over the visit, but people in —— seldom take off their coats if they don't have to.

Tess's loft is long and expansive. The main floor is wide with black couches and most of the focus collapsing on a white wall held adjacent to the floor-to-ceiling windows. Like animal magnetism. There are little silver placards on the wall where maybe art should go or has gone but it's not there now because it isn't finished or has been seen too much. Bell reclines on one of the couches. Her hair floats on her shoulders like duckweed. There are dark rings beneath her eyes like black puddles after the rain.

-This? Bell asks, gesturing toward me.

-This is Y, Tess says. Did you catch the game, Y?

-Most of it. Then I was on the subway. How did it turn out?

-20 to Nil, Bell says darkly. She rises from the couch and moves toward the kitchen. There are some voices in the kitchen and the radio is on.

-We blocked an extra point then? I ask Tess.

-Yes. For the last touchdown. The kick was blocked.

-I wish I had heard what Mildred had to say about that.

-Yes, Tess nods. It was very sad and very beautiful, but I can't quite remember it now. It was heroic, I think. In some small way. All that effort for the same result. A. Simpson, wasn't it? The nose guard. He blocked it. A field goal blocked, down 20/ nil. Astounding.

-Mm.

Voices emerge from the kitchen, carrying the radio that is now turned off. Four pale bodies with black hair of different lengths walk in a cloud around Bell. Bodies I have never seen before with alien faces. They split in the living room and diffuse toward the white door in the wall that leads to Tess's studio. The studio hides behind the display wall and once all the bodies are behind it, the wall seems like the surface of the harbor. We watch them huddle around each other through the open door. Bell keeps the radio in her arms and comes back into the living room.

-Our friend is reading tonight, Bell says. Do you typically listen?

-Sometimes, I say.

After the game, a secret cult of glitterati from somewhere in France, Kêr-Is, maybe, host different poets on a radio hour. Sometimes the poets talk about their families and if they're going to move out or not. They read their poetry in flat-blood drones where the words dip down beneath the shape of words into a soup of useless sound, directed at no one. It is the lukewarm bathwater of feeling and the words just cover up the pages used to plug the drain.

-The artists in the studio are preparing for the exhibition now, Bell tells me, meaning the bodies I'd just seen. They had just taken a break to drink a glass of water.

-I see.

-Just one glass of water between them, Bell clarifies. These artists, they share everything. They all share one name.

-Ah.

-Watching them work is very amazing.

-I'm sure.

Bell's eyes narrow, squeezing me between her eyelids. She sits back on the couch with her arms wrapped tightly around the radio. The radio does not seem to be on. I imagine the four pale artists with alien faces, their insect hands wrapped equally around the water glass. Their tongues flit against the water. They make mandalas out of garbage and clay. One has a very serious acid burn on their fingers, and so they all have very serious acid burns on their fingers now. Forty fingers. They must copy each other's wounds.

-Does he do anything? Bell asks Tess.

Tess looks at me like an insect in a glass of water.

-Do you do anything, Y? she asks. Like anything artistic?

I tell them I write sometimes.

-You write? Bell asks. Are you writing anything right now?

-Yes.

-Is it any good?

-No.

Bell pouts again. She was excited for a moment. Bell seems to me like one of those who eats art like communion wafers. The artists in the wall now are forging some half-sacrament. I look at Tess. Bell switches the radio on.

:elu on valu, elu on valu, elu on valu, elu on, elu on…

It is clear in —— that at last the monkeys have seized full control of every typewriter and every paint pen. The art machine will spin itself out with the same fuel it always has. The same desperations. Thin, blank, sun-stained, sunk-eyed, self-indulgent and faceless. The artists behind the walls are producing half-draperies, half-finished, half-maintained. Bugs drowning in the half-glass. I don't know where the money comes from for the loft. Sometimes I think it falls from the sky.

We watch through the open door in the wall as the artists take turns cleaning their ears with the same cotton swab.

-Isn't it beautiful, Tess? Bell asks. Isn't it divine?

-Yes, it's so beautiful, Tess says. And it's very divine.

-Isn't it original? Bell asks. Isn't it new?

-Yes, it's very brilliant, Tess says. And it's very new.

Bell turns her eyes to the blank wall like there's dinner in the kitchen. This may be the kitchen where Tess cut Ng's body up into thin canvas shards of imprint. Strips of meat on canvas thinly sliced. Trash bags in the harbor and maggots in the bag.

-Do you still paint, Tess? I ask.

Tess's face sinks very far away, falling out the window and into the deep black water down with the hulls of sunken subway cars. Bell seems to darken on the couch.

-No, says Tess quietly. I haven't painted for some time now.

There is silence on the radio. The silence is particularly loud. No doubt the poet has counted on the radio hum to take the place of silence and to be heard. The radio is its own whitewall, behind where the poet hides, only a small open door of voice to be seen through.

I met the secret cult of French glitterati a few months back in a warehouse on the outskirts and learned that none of them are French and very few of them are artists, outside a few black sketches laid down on the backs of bouncing checks. They are good people though. But this is the way of things in ——. No one is exactly. Dissonances of the soul and ego like radio waves in a subway tunnel.

-El went over Jersey, I say all at once.

-No...whispers Tess.

-Lil told me, I say. Earlier. I went to see her.

-That's two in one month.

-Who was the other one?

-You didn't know Wu?

I shook my head because I didn't. Tess looks out the window

again and very far away. The gold in her eyelids reminds me of the lock on my apartment door.

:*valu, valu, valu...valu...valu valu*

The poem is only a series of notes. There is an obsession in —— with repetition.

-I heard he ate a colander of gravel, Bell says darkly. Wu did. And then he went inside of a sauna and sat down. You can imagine how painful that must have been.

-Your insides start bleeding, Tess tells me, like she is reciting a piece of novel trivia she is proud to have obtained. Like the last name of a Japanese director or the hometown of a long-forgotten president.

-How did El go? Bell asks.

-I don't know. Lil didn't say.

-Maybe it's an infection, Tess whispers.

-Maybe.

-Or a parasite, Bell adds.

-Maybe.

The artists in the studio have begun rehearsing. I heard through the grapevine about what would be on display. When there is something to be known about Tess's exhibitions, everyone wants to know so that they aren't caught flat-footed and can have something to say.

The artists are fixing food in the microwave. They are making notes to see a doctor. They are reaching out to old friends from middle school. They are changing the water in the filter. They are clearing the smudges off the glass. In each action, they divide up the movements like lovers over the last piece of cake. When there are words to be said or written, they trade syllables in rotation. When one yawns or scratches or coughs, the others obey the motion. Bell, Tess, and I watch on through the rectangle of the doorway, seeing fractals of movement. The blank spaces on the walls where Ng's body was watch also. No one has much to say.

-Did you come here just to tell me that? Tess asks.

-No, I say. I went to see Ng first because Lil said they were close. Then he sent me your way.

At the mention of Ng's name, Bell rises up from the couch. I don't see what happens to her face. Maybe her cheeks flushed red with anger. Maybe her nose rotated in place like a clock adjusting for Daylight Savings Time. Maybe she stifled laughter. Maybe she ate her own lips before looking away.

-Is he still down at the Gymnasium? Tess asks.

-Yes

-Did you see him fight tonight?

-No

Tess sighs.

-It's hard to see your ex-husband do a thing like that.

-You were married?

-Does it change anything either way?

-Maybe it does. I don't know.

I think of the vows they might have said in a plastic cathedral. I think of Ng in a borrowed tux with his hair slicked down to his shoulders. I think of Tess clutching a bouquet of white roses, worried about the future, about Ng's temper, about all the ways one can mis-live a life.

-Maybe not.

:elu on...Elu...on! elu...elu!...elu...on...

Bell left the radio by the couch. It belches the same lines, then fades away.

-You were close? I ask.

-No, not really. Not in quite that way.

-Oh, I say. Still. It's hard to know someone who's gone over Jersey.

-Oh, I thought you were talking about Ng.

-No.

-Oh. I wasn't particularly close with El either.

-That's ok.

I think about asking if she's close to Bell now, but it seems like too much of an imposition. Especially with the artists trading strokes of sponge over a coffee mug in the studio sink.

-What is this then? I ask, changing the subject. The exhibition, what's it all about?

Tess sighs again. I have kicked her mind off like a squib kick blown down by the wind, somewhere out across the harbor. Her thoughts sink into the bay, swimming like a cat in a plastic bag, tangled in the wrap of Ng and El's face, whom she cannot recall. I can see the edge of the lighthouse blink in the distance, throwing beams of white light out over the water.

-Why don't you ask them? she says airily. We lost control of the exhibition a while ago. The art is growing in on itself now. Like spores. An invagination. The hyperreal. We no longer control the meaning. It has copied itself to the point of total abstraction.

I stare through the doorway to the studio a while to watch the artists dry their coffee mug. Their fingers curve delicately inside the handle, sopping the water that clings by surface tension to the bottom of the ceramic glass. Like pupas or maggots, their fingers move. Tess lifts a hand across her lips. Her eyebrows fold. I stand up and walk to the studio. Bell eyes me from the kitchen but makes no sound.

-What is this then? I ask the hoard of limbs by the sink. Their heads turn at once like a set of mirrors or faces when one suddenly enters a restaurant or lecture hall.

-Hec > at > on > cheire.

-Hecatoncheire?

-Yes, Bell says from the kitchen. It's Greek. It's Greek, from Greek mythology.

-The > Hec > at > on > cheires > hel > ped > Zeus> ov > er > throw > the > Ti > tans.

-Multi-headed, multi-handed, offspring of Uranus and Gaia, Bell explains.

-They look sad scooping coffee grounds out of the drain.

-What would you have them scoop?

-Yes, > What > would > you > have > us > scoop?

-I don't know, I shrug. Paper maybe.

-You're not guiding the exhibition, Bell scowls.

-I know.

The Hecatoncheire moves away from the sink and each flings a pinch of coffee ground into a metal trashcan. Then they sit together on a stool in the center of the room and begin passing around a cigarette, taking pigeon inhales. I think of the god in Ng's locker and of staying alive.

-Why not one of the Hindu gods? I ask. Why not Kali?

-Like the Kali Yuga?

-Yes.

-Wouldn't that be too...

-On > the > nose?

-I suppose so.

-Why does one go on brushing their teeth if they know they are going to die? Bell asks.

-How > many > times > will > you > brush > your > teeth > be > fore > your > time > to > die?

-I see now.

-One always feels more alone with others, Bell sighs.

I turn away from the studio to look at Tess. She is still sitting by the window on the very large couch, but she has brought her braids beneath her eyeballs and is crying. It is like being caught between the movements of two tectonic plates or train cars in a long and unfamiliar underground. In the studio, there is the wrath of the artists, the intersecting latices of metaphor, a bulb of some simpering light—the overthrowing of gods, and of fathers, of time itself. The suggestion of Kali Yuga, the age of destruction, coffee grounds, sitting in once place, in one room, intimately estranged and together. In the living room, Tess is crying. Which in most languages means there is something overflowing off the top. Or clawing toward the surface. It means less in —— but still, a man who whispers or sighs 'I'm on fire' carries dim flickers of the same sentiment as one who is screaming it.

-Don't you have any other questions? Bell asks.

-No, not really.

-Then please step away from the door.

I do. She moves past me inside and pulls the curtain closed. I imagine they are undressing now, but I don't know why I have that feeling. A lot of the art in —— is like this. Heaving wads of meaning at some indiscernible point in invented space and praying the tangles stick. I sit back down on the couch far away from Bell. She sees me and attempts to plug her eyes from crying.

-She made that up, you know? The Hecatoncheire part.

-Yes, I know.

-I thought it was about intimacy, you know. About other people.

-Yes. I had thought so too.

-Enough has been said about other people, I think. What do you think? Tess asks.

I don't think. I feel nauseated by the art here. I feel nauseated by the people also. I had begun feeling nauseous all the time and for a long time now. I wanted to find El because he was over Jersey and that was supposed to mean something. All these people weren't and they were in love or out of love and trying to say something about it. In repetitions. Like a virus.

-Other people exist to convince you that you aren't reading enough or fucking enough, I say at last. Tess smiles a wounded smile.

-You really do belong here, Y.

-Yes.

Tess sighs.

-Are you sad you came over?

-No.

-Are you sad more broadly?

-No.

-Are you ever sad?

-You shouldn't ask people so many questions.

-Why?

-You'll always know more about other people than they know about you.

-Isn't that always true?

-No. For some people, other people will always know more about them. Either because they talk too much, or they're the kind that people want to ask about themselves.

-Which are you? Tess says, sliding toward me on the couch.

-I am trying to settle my accounts.

-What does that mean?

-I am trying to know less about things than I know now.

-And how is that going?

-Poorly.

:elu on velu...elu on velu...elu! on! velu!

The curtain slides open again. The Hecatoncheire has changed into dark blue pajamas. They are sharing the same wooden toothbrush, passing it in a line between themselves after each brush. Bell stands in the doorway and scowls at me.

-Zed knew El, she mutters coldly. I think they were very close.

-Is that true? Tess asks her.

The cold look intensifies.

-Yes.

There is silence in my direction. The Hecatoncheire begins dribbling little strings of toothpaste spit from their lips. They reach to turn the water on. In bed, they will each read a single syllable from *Ali Baba and the Forty Thieves*, back and forth for maybe half an hour. It seems this is the fatal flaw of the exhibition. Bell has been experimenting with chloral hydrate, flurazepam, zopiclone, pentobarbital, and St. John's Wart to try and put the Hecatoncheire to sleep all at once. But still, there will be a moment. Maybe only space for two or three fragments of thoughts, when the heads are nodding off in order. Like a sting of lightbulbs burning out. Perhaps she should leave the exhibition with this imperfection. To drive the whole point home.

-Ok, I say. I'll find him.

-He works late, but he lives on the (3) line.

-That's far.

-We can call you a cab.

-No, that's alright.

-I already did.

-Oh. Thank you.

-Don't mention it.

Tess walks into the kitchen and comes back with an orange.

-You should eat something, she tells me.

-Do you have any apricots?

-No.

-Ok.

The two women walk me toward the door. Bell is more urgent, but Tess still looks sad. I wonder how they will be beside one another in bed tonight. I wonder if Bell realizes she is in the process of being wedged out. Hence the desperation. I wonder about Bell being next on the flat canvas floor of the Gymnasium, her teeth sewn in her mouth like the links of a bicycle chain. Everyone has got to learn sometime.

-Goodbye, Y, they tell me.

-Goodbye.

7.

Out on the sidewalk, the weather has turned. The wind from the harbor is no longer the same biting whip but has grown hot and muggy. That is how it is in ——. There are cults of mercury-drinking meteorologists who stand on the tops of tall buildings and send out text message alerts each time they believe the weather has turned. You can see the bulbs of their white balloons, floating out like dislodged eyeballs in the skyline. Perhaps the kind of balloon Cee had used when she went over Jersey. Perhaps that makes sense. It is hard to get a handle on life in ——. Perhaps because of the weather.

The street outside Tess's place is empty. An old man walks an old dog along a row of parked cars. The old dog spots a patch of mulch where a small dead tree points skyward. A Prairiefire Crabapple with its berries falling off. The old dog stands in the mulch but pisses directly onto the sidewalk instead. The old man looks up at the clouds, sticks his tongue out to check if it's raining. I can see that the man is blind. His glass eyes point off in opposite directions. A dusty white ice cream truck trundles down the street's median. It stops in front of Tess's place.

-You Y? the driver asks.

-Yes.

-You're going to Spruce Flats?

-Yes.

-I'm your ride.

I hesitate at the curb, but the driver seems used to the hesitation. There are black Xs over some of the ice cream bars advertised beside the truck's service window. I wonder if this means he's out of stock or if the ice cream bars aren't made anymore. The step-up on the other side of the truck is steep. The driver helps haul me inside.

-There's an alpaca blanket in the back there, he says. It can get kind of cold with the refrigeration.

-Thank you.

He nods. The driver is an older man with thick, hairy knuckles, and facial hair that looks like it was applied with charcoal. He looks to be from another century. Appearing in the mold of the gruff, domineering Baltic father. Progenitor to some sensitive, effete, Belarusian poet-author. The body one would see drunkenly clutching a belt in the frame of a bedroom doorway. Or shoulders protruding out from a rustic quilt, making brutal, unforgiving, passionate love to a doting, bonneted mother. The ice cream truck mutes him. Like catching one of these men at the funeral for an estranged acquaintance, belonging to a different religious sect. I lift the blanket over my shoulders and plant myself beneath him in the bucket seat. He forces the truck onward. The radio is still playing Poet Hour, but the poet has changed. The new poet has a wispy, broken voice.

:*Dans un bol melanger/ la chaire/ de crabe et le cream cheese.*

-Why do you want to go across town at this hour? he asks as we cut toward the turnpike.

-I don't.

-And yet you are.

-Yes.

-Doing what he doesn't want to, the driver muses. That says a lot about a man.

-Yes. I agree.

-Hm.

The driver strokes his beard. A thin layer of black dust comes off on his palm. He wears a thick brown leather coat and trousers like the bottom half of combat fatigues. In the back of the truck, Drumsticks, Fudgsicles, and Chocolate Eclairs rattle against the refrigeration like train cars on the flat of a freighter ship, waiting to be dumped into the sea.

-You have a familiar face, the driver tells me.

-I get that a lot.

-When people see you, they must think they've seen you before.

-Yes.

-It is an unenviable trait for one to have.

-Maybe. I have it for myself sometimes.

-Oh?

-Yes. In mirrors.

At a red light, the driver sifts through his pockets for a pouch of shredded tobacco and an old, smoke-stained billiard pipe. He packs a pinch into the chamber and holds the bit in his teeth. Having seen the Hecatoncheire, his fingers look alone. Isolated in their task. Disconnected.

:Ajouter les ingrédients restants un à la fois, en mélangeant soigneusement.

Before he can produce a match, the light turns green. The little pack of matches clatters to the floor.

-Some help? the driver asks.

I pick up the matches. They are flat and hard to light and I am afraid to disappoint him. I hold myself up against the dashboard as he leans the pipe toward me, his eyes still balancing on the road like tiny dark gyroscopes in his skull. The match ignites. The driver sucks hot wind beneath the tobacco. A black stream of smoke flows out from his nostrils.

-Thank you.

-Don't mention it.

He takes another pull and shifts the flame around. The truck begins smelling burnt and sweet. The wide window on the driver's side is open to let the smoke pour out.

-I was in the war, you know, the driver says.

-Which war?

-I was in Angola.

-Ah.

-The whole time...you would fuck your mother for a pinch

of good pipe tobacco.

-You would fuck your mother?

The driver gives me a strange look. I cannot tell what kind of conversation he expects us to be having.

-I would fuck yours too if it meant a good pipe, he says.

-That is really saying something.

-A man really says all he has to say.

-I suppose.

As we exit the on-ramp into the City turnpike, the driver begins impatiently switching between lanes. Each time, he cuts a little closer to the bumper in front or a little closer to the fender behind. Each time, he gives me a look like he's asking for approval. No one uses their horn in ——, and so there's no telling how the other drivers feel. Only the squeal of breaks, the rising entropy on the roadway. All the cars look like dilapidated bugs crawling in the same somber direction.

:*Étalez un wonton et mettre 1 cuillère à café du mélange dans le centre.*

-What kind of things did you do in the war? I ask suddenly, feeling it's what the driver is looking for. He lets off a large and inflected laugh.

-Many things, my friend. Many things.

The laugh percolates through the pipe smoke and gains a certain heaviness. I try pulling the alpaca blanket closer over my collarbones, trying to shield from the cloud.

-I was medic, he says. I know a lot about bullet holes.

-What can you tell me?

-Every bullet hole is like a woman.

-Yeah?

-They all have their own needs, their own...superstitions. But I will tell you a secret.

-Tell me.

-They all respect power.

-The bullet holes?

-Yes. Always remember that.

-I will.

The truck rumbles on. We are skating along the underside of the City. Here the buildings are tall, but on the other side, east of the highway, they begin to lessen. Spruce Flats, where Zed lives, is on the other end of downtown, away from the harbor on the City's south side. It used to be a hospital before it became luxury condominiums. Then when the luxury condominiums didn't sell, they carved up the units at cut rates and leased them out. The process was hasty. In some rooms, there are still obsidian chandeliers. In some rooms, there are still gurneys. Most of the tenants are emergency service workers or are employed by the City. There is a decrepit shawl hanging over Spruce Flats.

:*Humecter les bords avec de l'eau; plier en deux.*

-I used to have a young assistant in a field hospital in Dabiq, says the driver ruminatively. That is who you look like. I have been trying to place you. That is who you look like.

-Was he any good?

-No, not particularly, the driver mutters. He would tie the tourniquets too low. Many of the soldiers would end up bleeding out.

-That's too bad.

We have been in the same lane for the last ten minutes now, stuck behind a frozen foods truck. Perhaps the driver has calmed down. Often I feel like I have been reincarnated from the soul of a below-average civil servant who toiled away maintaining the flow of grain shipments in an obscure corner of an empire that had already fallen but where the news was slow to arrive.

-Have you ever watched anyone die before? the driver asks.

-No, but I have watched dead people.

-In the earth?

-No.

-In coffins?

-No. In the air above my bed.

-You're crazy.

-No, cursed.

-You shouldn't say crazy things.

-I'm not. You're telling me about the war. I'm telling you about the people above my bed. I put them there, you know.

-You're crazy. Quit being crazy.

-Alright.

The silence rots between us. The driver shifts the pipe in his mouth. The turnpike has slowed to a quiet hum. The buildings even on the east side are beginning to shrink in the direction of Spruce Flats. The frozen foods truck peels away before us.

:*Frire dans huile bien chaude environ.*

-Here I am trying to tell you about the real things in life. About war. And you want to be crazy.

-I didn't mean any disrespect.

-You couldn't disrespect me, the driver huffs. I would have to respect you for you to disrespect me.

-Let's not talk about it, ok?

-You couldn't disrespect me.

-I know.

-You couldn't.

-I know.

We pull off the highway. I know the driver has never been to war. Not because I have been to war, but just because I usually know when someone is lying. I don't feel bad for not asking more about the field hospital in Dabiq because it doesn't exist. To ask the driver to invent more about it would be cruel. Some people like to hear other people lie. But inside the heads of a liar, two worlds are splitting apart. They walk through life with their skulls split open, the two halves slamming unpleasantly against one another like the backs of train cars. I know this in myself and assume as much for other people.

When we start moving through the streets near Zed's apartment, I take off the alpaca blanket and sit on the truck's steps. I am seen by people on the sidewalks. Most are still caught wearing their heavy coats from when it was cold earlier and haven't bothered to take them off. Their faces sweat. They stand immobile on street corners, having forgotten where they planned to go. Dimly, they register they might want ice cream. Something in their skulls tells them they'd better not. It is hard to sell anything too indulgent in ——.

:*Égoutter sur du papier absorbant et laisser refroidir.*

-Almost there, the driver says.

-Yes.

-Poet's hour is almost up.

-Yes.

-Did you like the poetry?

I look back at the driver. His face is hiding something. Like a sneer has melted into the back of his two-half brain. The truck pulls to a stop outside of the main campus for Spruce Flats. The driver slides the throttle back into place.

-It's not poetry, I tell him. It's a recipe for Crab Rangoon.

-How about that.

-Yeah.

:*Servir avec la sauce aigre-douce ou avec une sauce piquante.*

I step out of the truck and onto the sidewalk.

The truck driver pulls off into the night.

8.

Zed lives at the far end of the old radiology wing at St Killian's South. When they were installing luxury condominiums here, they had tried turning the ward into a fitness center. Now the hallways are overwide and the walls are thin and hastily constructed. One can hear all the tapings of their neighbor's lives emanating through the plaster. The bristles of brushes rubbing on teeth. Bedframes creaking. Piss hitting the opposite side of the bowl. It is hard to imagine a man doing crunches in the ghost of an MRI machine here. Harder still to picture Zed and his son sleeping in the same echoes. The radiation that has seeped into the foundation from repeated use. The positrons and gamma rays. Decaying resounds of weakening magnetic fields. I knock on the door and slide my coat off into my arms.

-Hello, Y, Zed says in the doorway. We weren't expecting any company tonight.

-Hello, Zed. I wasn't either.

-I see. Would you come in?

I step through the narrow entrance and hang my coat on a hook in the hall. Zed is wearing a white smock over his plainclothes uniform. Even in jeans, it's clear he's a detective for the City. The swollen deltoids, clipped cop's haircut, the triceps give him away. Zed lives in a railroad flat where the thin rooms open back into one another. I follow him down the hall into the narrow kitchen. Little Zed stands on a stepladder, mushing teaspoons of imitation crab and cream cheese into unsealed wontons.

-Can you help? Big Zed asks.

-My hands aren't clean.

-Its ok. We're frying them anyway.

I nod and stand beside Little Zed. Little Zed's eyes are very big and brown and frightened. Little Zed hardly ever speaks except to say polite stock phrases. Yes Sir and No Sir and Thank You and Excuse Me.

-I have to do some work in the bedroom, Big Zed says. I'm supposed to go out tonight on a tour.

-Yes Sir, Little Zed says.

-Can you work the fryer, Y?

I look at a silver contraption on the kitchen's narrow sink. The gridded basket peers back at me like the frames of the cages at the Gymnasium. I look down at Little Zed and his small, sad eyes tell me that he knows how to work the fryer, but also knows someone larger than himself must cosign the operation.

-Yes, I tell Big Zed.

He gives a gruff nod and recedes through the doorway into the bedroom, untying his apron as he goes. Little Zed continues packing and folding wontons. Poet Hour is over now and there is a brief scheduled programming break. There is a bedroom beyond the kitchen and a bathroom beyond the bedroom and an open area beyond at the end of the apartment that I've never seen. Ng once told me that Zed manages to keep a CAT scanner back there. He has nurses from elsewhere in Spruce Flats come and operate it. He then mails the scans to Dot at the hospital. She draws circles on them with red wax pen and mails them back with diagnoses for a cut of the profits.

-Did you get this recipe from Poet Hour? I ask Little Zed.

-Yes Sir.

-Do you like Crab Rangoon?

-Yes Sir.

-Do you need me to help you pack the wontons?

-No Sir.

I know there are more complicated answers to these questions, but Little Zed has cut the world in two between Yes and No Sir. He has never had Crab Rangoon before. But on the whole, if Crab Rangoon is hearing the recipe on the radio, packing the crab and cream cheese clumps together, working the deep fryer, folding the wontons, then the answer is still 'yes.' Even if I'd asked 'do you like the *taste* of Crab Rangoon' or 'do you *want* me to help pack the wontons,' Little Zed could have dropped the question over the wedge of Yes and No Sir and come out with an answer. Big Zed has taught him to live this way. It is the way Big Zed lives. It is the language of a diagnosis. Of positive and negative replies. Nothing quantum. Nothing unsure.

In the bedroom, I can hear Big Zed sifting through paper. They are the thin kind of carbon papers the City uses for administrative tasks. Different cogs in the process receive a different color from the stack written by some far-off executor with ballpoint pen. Big Zed's papers are mostly blue and yellow. The writing on them is thin and very faded. He holds the pages up beneath a large incandescent desk lamp and copies the important parts onto a memo book he keeps in a pocket he's sewn into the calf of his pants. Next on WQQX is the radio drama story hour. Sometimes it's cowboys. Sometimes it's ghosts. Sometimes it's detectives.

-Do you listen to the radio drama story hour? I ask Little Zed.

-Yes Sir.

-Do you like it?

-Yes Sir.

-Do you ever turn off the radio when there are detective stories?

-No Sir.

-Do you ever think the detective in the story is your father?

Little Zed does not look up at me, but he begins packing the wontons faster. The little demitasse spoon slurps against the wet wonton edges, unloading cream cheese and crab. He uses his fingers to coat the creases and piles them all together onto a plate. The puckered lips of the wontons look like bloodless wounds under the kitchen light.

-Do you hope the story tonight is a detective story?

I can feel his little eyes trace upwards to the undercabinet radio where its sleek silver body clings to its nails in silence. The tiny blue numbers peer back, bent and contorted like broken bones snapped in set configurations. The soundless FM signals from WQQX pour through the kitchen like x-rays in a CT scan, soaking into the walls. There are tiny bald patches on Little Zed's head that I find concerning.

-No Sir, Little Zed says softly.

I watch as he removes the mesh basket from the deep fryer and loads in the wontons. He pulls down a tin container of cooking oil from one of the upper cabinets, straining on his toes on his stepladder. He unscrews the oil cap and pours the yellow mixture into the fryer. He gestures toward the button on the fryer to turn it on.

-Will there be enough time? I ask him.

-No Sir.

-But we'll try anyway?

-Yes Sir.

I peer a little longer into the oil. The wonton balls seem a little too much like skin. It has the feeling of a summary execution. Of a mass grave, somewhere in Dabiq or ——'s inner harbor. I wonder which of the wontons Little Zed tied too high or too low like the fictional young field medic. I press the button. Little Zed lowers the wontons into the oil. Deep foreboding saxophone music leaks from the radio above this hiss of frying skin. Drums crash ominously.

:*Stories in time and space...told in future tense!*

-It's the detective stories, I say.

-Yes Sir.

Little Zed pulls a small tube of Polynesian sauce from the refrigerator and begins setting the orange liquid into tiny plastic cups. The Narrator is describing the scene. All of the detective stories on radio drama story hour are about Detective X. Detective X is always in the hire of some large corporation trying to foil or complete an act of corporate espionage. Sometimes a murder. It is hinted at in the radio plays that Detective X is not one person, but many people, who all die, who all carry on the title, who are all dispensed listlessly back and forth in a lacunae of successions between scions of the corporate world. In the other room, Big Zed is putting his boots on. He is sliding his badge over his neck and slipping into his leather jacket. Little Zed checks the wontons and stirs the oil with a spoon.

:*You're just in the nick of time, Detective. Boy do we have a caper for you...*

-Pick one, Big Zed says from the doorway. He is holding out a stack of yellow papers, fanned to the side like the folds in a hospital gown. Like rows of scattered teeth.

-What are they? I ask.

-Warrants.

-Oh.

I reach out and pull one of the pages to the left side of Big Zed's thumb. There is a name on the paper and some signatures and some bold-text legal writing. The man in the small photograph in the corner of the page looks back at the camera with wilted eyes. His head is shaved and the edges of black tattoos creep up his neck. Big Zed takes the other warrants, folds them, and slides them into the breast pocket of his coat.

-Time to go, Little Zed.

-Yes Sir.

Little Zed turns the fryer off and strains the oil into the sink. Big Zed is walking down the hallway to the front door, leaving me holding the warrant page as Little Zed dabs oil off the partially fried wontons. He stuffs paper towels into a plastic container, outlining small spaces for the cups of Polynesian sauce to sit in.

:*Listen here, X. If those fat cats at Vista-Corp think they can just fleece our prototype without us standing up for ourselves, they've got another thing coming...*

Little Zed dumps the wontons into the plastic container and pulls me toward the door. Detective X is being tasked with recovering a prototype for a machine that allows for spectral bilocation. Big Zed takes Little Zed's coat off one of the hooks in the hallway and helps him slide into the sleeves. I take my coat down off the wall also and hold it like wet flesh.

-It's hot now, I say.

-Might not be later.

-That's true.

Big Zed opens the door out into the hallway. We can hear voices beyond the walls. Radio drama story hour seeps dimly inside the sound of flossing, conversations about dishwasher parts, the hum of laundry machines, arguments about wine stains left on throw rugs, and dirty dishes being placed back inside kitchen cabinets. It is a normal Tuesday night elsewhere in —— and the din of noises at Spruce Flats are the tantric ohms of the entire City. Each task, even the arguments, are done knowing they will have to be done again and again and it is only that again-ness that separates here from Jersey. We walk past a row of free-weights in the hallway. Objects that emanate repetition. Another method of keeping sane. Cigarettes for the body.

At the end of the hallway, an elevator opens to take us down to the parking lot. Little Zed stands between Big Zed's legs. Radio drama story hour plays in the elevator.

:Say, Spiff, isn't that one of the chief programmers for Vista-Corp? What's he doing in a dive like this?

The doors open. The white shine of lights in the parking garage is blinding. Like the hallways in the Gymnasium. I shield my eyes and take Little Zed's hand as he leads us through the elevator and out toward Big Zed's car.

-You never told me why you were visiting, Big Zed says, unlocking the back door of his black Crown Vic and piling Little Zed into a booster seat.

-I was here about El, I tell him.

-What about him?

-He went over Jersey.

The seatbelt pulls tightly over Little Zed's chest. Big Zed straightens. In the blinding light, I can only see the outline of his skull, tinged in white along the tiny shaved hairs of his scalp. He stands very still.

-Were you close? I ask.

-No, Big Zed murmurs. But my husband, you know.

-Yes.

-It's hard to hear about people going over Jersey.

-Always.

-Especially...

He looks down at Little Zed. Big Zed's husband, Lou, had gone over Jersey six months prior. He had made himself a hat out of the *Propædia* section of the Encyclopedia Britannica and used it to drown himself in the bathtub, face down.

-I'm sorry, I say. Bell told me you were very close.

-We weren't, Zed says. But I think Dot was.

-She's at the hospital still?

-Yes.

We don't say anything. I see myself reflected glumly back in the frames of Big Zed's aviators. I think about how thin I look. I feel like I should be carrying something. A card, maybe. Or a bouquet of flowers. Something to distract from the way I don't fit my clothing anymore. The only things I have in my pocket are my cell phone, my radio, and the Politician's campaign pin. They would not be enough to keep me from floating.

-I can give you a ride, Big Zed says at last. Or I can have one of the other guys in the squad take you there after I execute the warrant.

-Thank you. I appreciate that.

Big Zed nods. I move around to the other side of the Crown Vic. Little Zed is in the back seat, popping half-fried wontons into his mouth and sipping on the little cups of Polynesian sauce, mixing the contents quietly between his teeth. Big Zed turns on the car and the radio bursts on with a series of gun shots.

:*Zounds! He's getting away! / Goddamnit, Spiff, don't you think I can see that?*

Little Zed flinches at the gun shots. Big Zed pulls the car out of the parking garage, past rows of black and gray Honda Civics, Toyota Corollas, dented Ford Mustangs. The streets outside Spruce Flats lay empty. All of the nurses are gone to midnight shifts. The detectives are out on tour. It has started to rain.

-Why did Bell say I knew him? Zed asks.

-I don't know. I think maybe she was trying to get me to leave.

-Why would that make you want to leave?

-Because I feel like I'm looking for him, I say. Everyone seems to think they knew who knew him. I'm just trying to see who's right.

-That's a tough game.

-Yes.

-And how's the exhibit looking?

-It's about a bunch of arms, I say. Something like that.

Zed nods. I don't know where we're going, but I can tell he's not planning on taking the ordinary routes. Highways make Zed nervous. He takes left and right turns and meanders in the direction of downtown, curving and cutting through dark blocks of old rowhomes and public housing terraces. Tenants sit out on their stoops holding week-old newspapers across their eyebrows and looking up at the moon. Old ladies drag heavy plastic grocery bags in each hand. They make their ways up the block, turn around, and head back down to the other end.

-Any advice here? I ask him. For what I'm doing?

Zed grunts. Detective X is chasing someone down a fire

escape now. His loafers slip over the wet metal. Lightning bolts litter the sky. He reaches out for the perp's jacket. He grabs him. He holds him over the edge. The fire escape shakes with the thunder.

-There are no shortcuts in this, Y. You have to follow the string to its end.

-Is that what you did for him? I say, holding up the warrant page. Zed looks over at me from behind his sunglasses.

-Some strings are shorter than others, he mutters. That's just how it is.

-And his?

Zed sighs. His lips flap with his breath. At a stop sign, he glances back to where Little Zed has finished eating.

-Are you finished eating, Little Zed?

-Yes Sir.

:Listen, maggot, the Bishop Group has a lot riding on that prototype. Now we can do this the easy way, or by God, we can—

There is the sound of a loud thunk. The car starts moving again. Detective X is hit hard over the head with something dense and metal. He's out cold. The clouds above the Crown Vic begin swelling blue and pink with light pollution from downtown.

-What's bilocation anyhow? I ask.

-One person, two places at the same time.

-There's a lot of people like that, aren't there.

-Around here? Sure.

-You know what wonton means in Cantonese? I ask.

-No.

-It means 'swallowing clouds.'

-Huh, Big Zed mutters.

-You know what it means in Mandarin?

-What?

-Chaos.

Big Zed takes us onto one of ——'s main thoroughfares. The

--

road lies mostly empty outside of a few vacant busses making routine stops. The rain has pushed people inside their rooms for the night. Detective X wakes up to find he's been tied to a radiator.

:*You'll never stop us, X. Even as we speak, I'm meeting with the shareholders at the Vista-Corp right now. The prototype is ours. Come market open tomorrow, the Bishop Group will be nothing but a puddle of red left on the NASDAQ!*

The Crown Vic pulls to rest beneath the neon marquis of a large movie theater. A huddle of gray overcoats shoot dice by the door. All the movie theaters in —— play reruns of WQQX radio programs overdubbed with footage of the Grand Canyon. There was a consumer initiative a few years back to change the screening footage to stills of Dutch tulip fields, but the ballot initiative never gained traction. A lot of politicians lost their terms.

-I need you to pull the car around back, Big Zed says. He might make for the fire exit.

-And you're sure he's in there?

-Positive.

-How do you know?

-I know.

Big Zed piles out of the car, leaving the keys in the ignition. I follow him into the rain and stand in front of the Vic for a moment as Big Zed waits beneath the marquis. He pulls his collar up and skulks around the fringe of the dice game for an opening. I watch him fade the shooter. Most people in —— fade the shooter. The shooter rolls 9, then immediately out 7s. He sighs and hands each of the other gray men a loose wad of tangled bills. Big Zed takes his bills to the ticket counter. I turn back to the car.

-Did you know he would do that? I ask Little Zed.

-Yes Sir.

-The City doesn't pay for expenditures?

-No Sir.

-There's always something getting in the way.

-Yes Sir, says Little Zed.

On the radio, Detective X is using the crown of his wristwatch to saw through the zip-ties on the radiator. The CEO of Vista-Corp is opining about best practices for corporate governance. The jargon is complex and his explanation yields into the tall grass of arbitrage. The gray men in the dice game are all sitting bank presidents. They come down here on Tuesdays to play with more favorable odds. I pull the Vic back out onto the street.

9.

In the back alley behind the movie theater, tarps have been set up. White tents house the wares of a small, receding flea market. The proprietors are closing down. The crowd is leaving. I pull the Crown Vic to park beneath the faded red glow of the back exit sign and turn off the engine, leaving the radio on. The rain has thinned out for now.

-Do you want anything from the flea market, Little Zed?

-No Sir.

-Are you sure?

-Yes Sir.

-They might have some toys there.

Little Zed doesn't say anything. He turns his wide eyes out to watch the clouds clear away with the rain. I almost ask *do you want any toys* but figure the answer will be similar. Detective X escapes the zip-ties while the CEO's back is turned. He picks up a nearby metal folding chair and uses it to brain the CEO. The radio narrator describes the injury in graphic detail. He describes the CEO of Vista-Corp's intraparenchymal hemorrhaging. Retinal detachment. Subarachnoid hematoma and vasospasm. The pressure of blood squeezing down on his parietal lobe as his life fades to black. An injury like that leaves the injured dying in darkness.

-They didn't need to go into that much detail, I say.

-No Sir.

-Do you see injuries like that on the CAT scan?

-Yes Sir.

-From living people?

-Yes Sir.

-Huh.

:*I've got to get to that convention center, STAT! That presentation simply cannot go live! But someone has to save, Spiff...Drat! If only*

one man could be in two places at once...
-This one isn't very good, is it?

-No Sir.

-Do you think I have time to check on the flea market?

Little Zed cranes in his booster seat. His eyebrows furrow as he stares at the exit door. He looks at the proprietors loading up their shops into the backs of camper vans. He looks at the patrons in duster jackets seeping out of the alley back into the street.

-Yes Sir.

I nod. I leave the car on and step toward the last few remaining tents and tables. There are a few small puddles gathered in the alleyway like the holes of excavated eye sockets. The proprietors are mostly selling old radio players, marionette dolls, and ballerina shoes. I see a man who looks familiar standing beside a set of antique green glass bottles. It's Peanut from the Gymnasium.

-Hey Peanut, I say.

-Hey yourself.

-How's business coming.

-Almost sold out.

-That's good.

-Yep.

-How was the Gymnasium tonight?

-Quieter than usual. I think that's safe to assume.

-Any reason?

-People are tired, I suppose.

-That's probably true.

Peanut has started folding his bottles into foam swaddling and loading them up into dishwasher trays. He picks up a full tray and totes it over to his conversion van before walking back to his tarp.

-Is that the van they use for the fighters? I ask.

-No, that's my brother's van.

-It looks the same.

-Yeah. It does. He likes doing things like that. But look here.

I follow the end of Peanut's crooked finger to where it's pointing.

-The tailpipe is dented in on this one.

-Isn't that dangerous?

Peanut shrugs. The exhaust pipe resembles his finger. I look back at the Crown Vic to see Little Zed's face pressed against the glass. His breath leaves condensation stains in a clouded circle around his mouth.

-What brings you to the alley anyway? Peanut asks.

-I'm following Zed on a warrant.

-Oh. I better get moving then.

-Why's that?

-I think there's a paper out on me.

-Anything serious?

He shrugs again and begins packing up the bottles a little faster. The foam swallows each bottle he packs away. I think of the busted homemade single-barrel shotgun he's rumored to carry and I think about the crushed exhaust pipe. It makes sense that who owns both would be the man tasked with working the door at the Gymnasium.

-You can take one if you'd like, Peanut says.

-One of the bottles?

-Sure.

-I don't think I need one.

-You never know.

I nod and pick up one of the bottles. I hold it up and look through the dusted glass at the movie theater's exit signs. The red shards of light swirl inside the clouded green diaphane. Peanut takes the last of the dishwasher trays to his van and shuts the back door.

-That's a good one, he says. You made a good choice.

-I hope so.

-You did.

-I'm glad.

-Well, Peanut sighs, casting a vacant look around the alleyway. I'll be seeing you around then.

-Yeah, sure, I say. See you around.

Peanut gives a little nod. I notice the scar on his nose as he turns away. His van starts with a muffled choke. A cloud of black exhaust puffs off the van's tail pipe as he pulls out through the alley. There's a backfire like a shotgun burst. I think about Ms. Tupelo for a moment. Little Zed backs away from the window. I stand outside the Crown Vic massaging the empty bottle and the warps in the glass. The rain is very thin and small. The exit door to the movie theater slams suddenly open.

Big Zed has his arm slung around the man from the warrant and is leading him out of the doorway. The man is doubled over and has his hand plastered to the right side of his gut. The tattoos on the man's neck shake with frantic breathing. Big Zed gives me a pained look as he leads the man to the hood of the Vic. I shove the bottle into my coat.

-He's shot, says Big Zed.

-Did something happen?

-No, Big Zed says. We were talking about guns and I forgot I had the safety off.

-It's my fault, really, the wounded man grunts. I should have known better.

-It's ok now. I think the bullet went right through. Full metal jacket.

I help Big Zed lay the man onto the hood of the Vic as Big Zed applies pressure to the wound. Blood is spreading through his laced fingers. The wounded man's shirt is getting wet. The blood looks lighter than it should in the glow of the exit sign. Like the man himself is leaking neon.

-I've called for a medevac, but we've got to get him to a rooftop, Big Zed says.

-Is there one nearby?

-Yes, but we should probably hurry. Help me put him in the backseat. I'll keep applying pressure. Little Zed, can you sit up front?

-Please turn the radio on, the wounded man says.

-It's on, I tell him.

-Ok, I'm ready to go then, he whispers.

We move him clumsily into the backseat, crumpling him up and then laying him flat over the vinyl. Little Zed offers up his coat as a bandage. It is not a very good tourniquet, but I suppose there are no tourniquets for gut shots.

-Will he make it? I whisper to Big Zed.

-Maybe, he tells me. It's a sucking chest wound.

-Oh.

Big Zed crawls into the backseat beside the wounded man and keeps applying pressure. I climb back onto the driver's side. Little Zed looks small and numb beside me in the passenger seat, coatless, pulling the safety belt over his thin shoulders.

-Take a left when you get out of the alley, Big Zed says.

-Alright.

:Forget it, Mr Chairman. Your engineers will never be able to forge a copy of the prototype. The Bishop Group's patent lawyers will have you up to your eyeballs in infringement actions!

-Take another left at the next light, Big Zed says.

-Sure.

-What's the prototype of? asks the wounded man.

-It's a bilocation device, I tell him.

-Oh.

The stoplights have all started blinking yellow in ——. I press down on the gas and maneuver the Vic around slow-moving taxi cabs, flower delivery vans, and ice cream trucks. The windshield wipers swish over the glass like insect legs. The wounded man begins to softly moan.

:Very clever, X. But we'll see what Vista-Corps friends on the 9th

Circuit have to say about that. In the meantime, don't you have some predators to worry about? And I don't mean investors!

A trap door opens beneath Detective X, and he drops into a pit of red-tailed boa constrictors. One of the snakes coils itself around his neck.

-He's done for, the wounded man whispers.

-No Sir, says Little Zed.

-Bilocation?

-Yes Sir.

-Hm.

-It's that one on the right, says Big Zed. The glass one.

-I don't know how to parallel park, I tell him.

-It's ok. Just run it up on the sidewalk then.

The Crown Vic hops the curb. We pile out of the car together. Big Zed drags the wounded man out by his feet before slinging him over his shoulder. The tiny sleeves of Little Zed's coat hang over Big Zed's neck as we head for the building's lobby. Something about the blood and the wounded man makes the scene shaky and unreal. The sucking chest wound has pulled some of the surrounding reality inside it, numbing the edges of perception. Trapping the perimeters within his gut. I think about the drain in my bathtub.

Inside, the desk guard is staring out the window and listening to the radio. He stands up to meet us. His face is very young, but his eyes are hollowed far back into his head like puddles in an alleyway. He wears a black sweater vest. Blood drips onto the marble floor in the vacant lobby.

-We need to use the elevator, Big Zed says. I'm a detective.

-Alright, says the desk guard.

We all move to the elevator. The desk guard slides a key into a slit beneath the silver buttons. His fingers are long and elegant like the fingers of a concert pianist.

-It takes a while, he says. The elevator has to perform emergency functions.

Big Zed nods. The wounded man continues to bleed into his shoulder. Little Zed gazes down the massive corridor and sticks his hands in his tiny pockets.

-What do they do in this building? I ask the desk guard.

-Health insurance, mostly. Life insurance too.

-Oh.

-Is he badly hurt? the desk guard asks.

-Yes Sir, says Little Zed.

The desk guard looks suddenly sad. The glowing numbers above the elevator begin counting backward, descending rapidly.

-We're meeting a medevac though, I tell him.

-That's good.

The elevator arrives, and we step inside. The desk guard twists his key and the doors close shut again. WQQX is playing inside the elevator, but the show has gone to credits. The narrator is reading a list of disjunctive names and their set assignments.

-Maybe he really did die, the wounded man groans.

I look down at Little Zed, but he doesn't say anything. He holds Big Zed's bloody hand as the elevator ascends. I imagine the shoes of all the little insurance executives stepping over the residue of the wounded man's blood. I imagine their little heads crowded together, their arms by their sides, their ties like pendulums. I think about the Lernaen Hydra. I think about the Hecatoncheire. The gunshot wound continues siphoning reality from the elevator as the numerical buttons begin resembling the silver skin of Azrael. The angel whose body is made entirely of eyeballs and tongues. Whose number matches with the number of souls inhabiting the earth. It seems the elevator is flooded with numbers now on all sides but the numbers are turned off. The elevator is accelerating. We reach the top floor.

The elevator opens directly on the rooftop where the medivac is waiting. Two men dressed in canvas-colored uniforms hop out of the helicopter. The helicopter is dark green and looks like it belonged to the military. We help load the wounded man onto a gurney the medevac operators wheel over. The helicopter blades whip up a gust of wind, and I can see where the clumps of hair on Little Zed's head have fallen out.

-We'll take it from here, the medevac unit tells us, strapping the wounded man onto the stretcher.

Big Zed nods. His shoulder is covered in the wounded man's blood and the features of his face have become unsteady. The chest wound must have sucked the distinction from them. He looks like a face one forgets on the train. A little like mine.

-I'm sorry, Y, he says. This didn't go as expected.

-It's ok.

-I feel bad about the gun.

-Yeah. These things happen.

We watch as the medevac unit lifts the stretcher and hoists it over toward the helicopter. Big Zed looks away.

-They'll probably take you to the hospital if you want.

-You think so?

-Ask them.

-Ok.

I put my arms over my head and move through the wind of the chopper blades. The medevac unit is strapping the wounded man onto the floor of the helicopter now. The one closest to the door glances back at me. The men in the helicopter look a bit like spelunkers in their uniforms, preparing for descent. I shout something about the hospital. He shrugs and sticks out his arm. The door slides shut behind me.

10.

We leave Big Zed and Little Zed standing on the rooftop together beside the helipad. Little Zed's bare arms shiver in the wind. Big Zed covers him up with his bloody jacket and leads him back toward the elevator.

The medevac operator not flying the helicopter uses a long, thin needle to perform a chest decompression on the wounded man. They've sealed over the gunshot and hooked the man into a breathing apparatus. The wound is sealed on three sides, leaving space for the air in the sucking wound to escape.

-X really got the short end on that one, didn't he? the pilot says into his headset mic.

-You don't think he bilocated? says the medic.

-Nah, the snakes got him.

-What about Spiff?

-Spiff stays Spiff, says the pilot. That's the secret. He had the real bilocater on him the whole time. It was Spiff who knocked X out on the fire escape. Spiff was probably shorting Vista-Corp stock the whole time. Let them think they had the real prototype for a quick bounce on the Hong Kong markets, then use the bilocater to get to his broker just as X crashed the board presentation. Insider trading.

-Same Spiff, different Xs?

-Funny that way, isn't it?

-House always wins.

The helicopter begins lift off. The blades chop faster as the pilot pulls at levers and nobs on the panel of controls. Needles twist against the faces of various dials. The medic hands me a radio helmet and points to a bucket seat by the window. The ground begins drifting away. The pilot presses down on one of the floor petals and the copter rotates away from the helipad.

Beneath us, ——'s skyline reaches up like stalagmites into

the blackened sky. The rain here has dripped the buildings into being. Jagged metal teeth punctured with fine holes of light and empty windows. Like needlepoints stuck through iron lanterns. The sucking wound from the man's chest is leaking excess reality back into the helicopter cabin, and I become acutely aware of the curving of my own fingers. I watch my thumbs performing Kara Nyasa involuntarily. I think of the Palimistrist saying I have disgusting palms. There is no use in purification, but the fingers are moving anyway. Gestures in the dark.

-Hey buddy, the medic says, tapping my knee. What's the guy's deal? You know?

-Zed shot him, I say.

-For real?

-Looks so.

-He's got exit wounds in two places. Like the gun was fired twice from inside him.

-That's strange.

-Well. You know what they say about bullet wounds.

-No.

-Every bullet wound is like a man, the medic tells me. They've all got something stupid to say.

-Huh.

The wounded man's eyes drift open. His pupils float absently to the window, projecting out against the sky. His hair is wispy and gray. There is dried blood peeling off of his lower lip. His mouth is held open in an O shape like the outlines of a yantra. I think he looks pretty good for someone dying. Not attractive, but just like how someone dying should look.

-You mind if we listen to the radio? the pilot asks.

-No, not at all.

-We like listening to the recap, he explains.

-Go right ahead.

After radio drama story hour on WQQX, a discussion of the program is hosted by a panel of theorists from the community college. The panel is composed of a rotating cast, but the lenses they hold remain generally consistent. The Eternal Spiff theory, or the Variable X theory, is pretty doctrinal. But it gets more complicated with the ghost and cowboy dramas. There is great disagreement over the finer geodesics of the story universe. Some of the experts maintain that radio drama story hour recurs within one frame of Being. Like echoes. Others are not as convinced.

:*What we see in Detective X, rather, what we phenomenologically experience, is a figure at rest on the plane of immanence. A shell without haecceity, without potentialities, a projection...*

The medic finishes affixing the wounded man to the suitcase EKG machine. He takes out a blue notepad and scribbles down preliminary vitals. The machine reads out a slow series of blinking neon lines. Blue. Green. Orange. The steady beeping makes an involuntary percussion with the hum of the copter blades.

-Are we far out? I ask him.

-No. Not so far out. We have to bend over the harbor though. We can't fly directly through downtown.

-City ordinance, says the pilot.

-Ah.

The helicopter is curving slowly away from the inner city, heading east out toward the bay. There is nothing distinct about the tallest buildings downtown. I think in other cities they use those buildings to staff the interiors of snow globes or shape the silhouettes they put on t-shirts, but in —— there is no architectural flair. The tallest buildings are only tall in the general mold of the shorter buildings around them. As if some foreign center of gravity has just happened to pull their rooves further away from the earth. Like lunar tides. As if by accident.

:*...and as for the semiotic linguistic landscape of the story, it speaks to the professor's conceptualization of the dramas as generative systems. Like the fire escape, for example. If we are to entertain fully*

the diachronic reading, I think keeping in mind the prospect of a fully
generative system is exegetic.

-You've known Zed long? the medic asks.

-Maybe 6 months.

-You heard about his husband?

-Yes.

-You think he did it?

-Did what?

The pilot glances back at the medic. The medic recedes from
the wounded man and sits in the bucket seat diagonal from me
on the other side of the cabin. He takes out an anxiety cube,
a six-sided dice with different fidget functions, and begins
massaging a switch with his fingers.

-The *Propædia* section isn't all that heavy, he says.

-He was very thin.

-Still.

-You think Zed tied it onto him?

-I think the man attracts death.

-That's a lot to say about a person.

-I think I have my proof.

Downtown rotates slowly away from us. Through the cockpit,
I can see ——'s dockyards on the outskirts of the harbor begin
sifting steadily into view. Fields of stacked shipping containers
appear huddled together through curtains of low-hanging
clouds. The upturned legs of yellow cranes. Half-constructed
freighter vessels waiting alone in the crevices of dry docks. A
haze of water droplets forms on the windshield and is scraped
away.

-Few months ago, the medic starts, we got a call out to a
property on the west side. Another warrant. The woman he was
after barricaded herself inside her home with her four young
children.

-I can see where this is going.

-You'd think. But it wasn't her fault. While she was in there, her home suffered a gas leak. Freak occurrence. Something had dented the CNG hose on her washer-dryer. All five people inside the home died of carbon monoxide poisoning before we arrived. We found the detective vomiting in a birdbath when we got there.

-These things happen, don't they?

-Not frequently. 18 people died in the country last year from gas leaks. Five of them were in ——.

-We might be cursed like that.

-Cursed, yeah.

-You should try some cleansing, that's all, murmurs the pilot. Maybe an egg.

-If you're superstitious like that, the medic adds.

I look down at the wounded man. His eyes have tilted up toward me and his neck is arched back. He is trying to lift his hand.

-Can't afford not to be, I sigh.

The medic nods. He twists the fidget cube over and begins pressing a set of useless buttons in geometric sequence.

:Or right, but to pick up on a different hermeneutic phrasing, I should say the Detective, or collective Detectives, suggest an embodiment, and indeed, a problematization of the always-already. And it is the same question of preceding noumena the professor raised last week with Sheriff Jake...

The fingers on the wounded man's hand begin beckoning toward me. The medic is still absorbed in his cube. Out the widow, we've nearly reached the edge of the harbor. Out where the city lights are reflected in the dark. The shimmering gleam gazing back at us.

-You...the wounded man whispers.

-Me?

-You.

I slide out of my seat and onto the metal floor of the cabin. I can feel the shaking of the helicopter as I lean my head closer to the wounded man. The open hole of his mouth rises to eye level. He turns his head.

-Can you do something with a message? he asks me.

-I don't know.

-Can you try?

-Sure.

His eyelids flutter. His breathing has become thick and muddy. I look at the EKG readout but the lines are meaningless. The peaks continue on in steady occurrence, rising and falling back again. Like buildings raised arbitrarily over empty plains.

-It's about the City, he says. The City apparatus.

-Is it political?

-In a way.

-Is it why they were after you? With the warrant?

-No, the wounded man says. I was stealing automobiles.

-Why?

-It's not related.

-Ok.

The wounded man blinks heavily. I think the medic sees me, but I'm not sure. He twists his cube over again and begins spinning a metal ball bearing.

-It's in my coat pocket, the wounded man says. Can you find it?

-I'll try.

I begin rooting through his coat pocket. There are clots of spare wiring and lock picks crowding the pouch. The pocket is also still a little wet with blood. My fingers brush across a folded piece of paper. I pull it out from the fabric.

-Don't open it! coughs the wounded man. Not until it's the right time.

-When will it be the right time?

The wounded man sits up slightly to look at me. His eyes are blue and especially clouded. He looks at me like I've said something totally meaningless. Like when someone raises their hand to say something irrational in a crowded room. The EKG machine begins beeping wildly. The vital lines curl and dip into a triple helix of symbols. The numbers on the machine cycle sporadically. The medic springs from his chair.

I fall back against the door as the medic's hands flit over the wounded man's body. He attends to different fixtures in the ventilator and pulls out another decompression needle. He stares at the long thin metal and glances back at the EKG. A shade of resignation passes over his face. He digs the needle in.

:And thus, to suggest the full landscape of the dramas symbiotically relates to a 'Ship of Theseus' is apt, but I would postulate there is a certain tathātā at play, sine qua non. Such an indulgence desires a more fractally infused thus-ness than the professor's analysis of X implies.

The wounded man sucks in a final gust of air. The lines on the EKG machine all fall flat together at once. There is a low, continuous beeping that spreads throughout the cabin. I look up at the medic.

-Tension pneumothorax, the medic says. That was an injury he should have survived. But for the curse of Zed.

-Should I take us out over the harbor? the pilot asks softly.

-Yes. I'll get the sealant.

I watch as the medic takes a thick syringe filled with a black, viscous liquid from one of the interior cabinets. He removes the dead man's bandage and applies the liquid to the puncture wound. The chopper strafes right, taking us further out over the water. I fold the dead man's note a second time and slide it deeper into my pocket.

-You should strap in, the medic tells me. Just in case.

-I wish we didn't have to do this, says the pilot. It's always awkward at the hospital.

-I think with Zed, they'll understand.

-The CNO has been weirdly concerned about fuel cost lately. I think they're thinking of shutting us down.

10.

-They're always thinking of shutting us down, says the medic. They never do.

The medic undoes the straps on the dead man's gurney as the City pan's back into view. The pilot stabilizes the chopper in the direction of downtown. The reticulum of yellow windows stares back at us through the cockpit's windshield like the eyes of a bug. The medic pulls the gurney toward the chopper door and slides it open. The chopper cabin fills with wind.

-Do you want to say anything? the medic yells.

-Akal! I shout back through the slapping air. Akal!

Our words are taken away by the harbor. The medic shrugs. He drops into a squat position beside the gurney and hoists the dead man up. The dead man's body slides off the gurney, over the helicopter edge, and down into the water. I watch as he plummets. His arms stretch out beside him, but not in any meaningful way. It is a few seconds until the body hits the surface. There is very little splash. The medic pulls the door closed, shutting out the wind.

-We have to put that sealant on them when we dump them in the harbor, the medic says. It's procedure. With that kind of sucking wound.

-Oh.

-I'm sorry you had to see that.

-It's ok. I understand.

The medic nods solemnly and returns to his chair. He pulls out his anxiety cube and begins listlessly spinning the dial, staring pensively out the window. I think about wontons and swallowing clouds. I think about flesh frying in the thick oil of harbor water. I think about the dead man's wound becoming unsealed and sucking in the entirety of the bay. Maybe that's what they were trying to avoid with the sealant.

:And following that suggestion, we can see a certain deterritorialization grasped at the horizons of X, contrasting to the deeply entrenched, territorialized Spiff. Even if we continue in the

vernacular of recurrence, X is undoubtedly an iteration of objet petit a.

The chopper dips away in the direction of St Killian's North. We are not very far away.

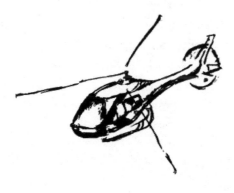

11.

On the helipad at the hospital, the medic reaches out to shake my hand. The blades of the chopper are slowing down now like the sound of mechanical whirring being sucked through a faucet. The pilot stands at the edge of the hospital roof, smoking a cigarette. The façade of the hospital faces out into the harbor while the downtown skyline recedes behind us like the lapping of a tall swell.

-We'd appreciate you not telling anyone about this, says the medic.

-I won't.

-These procedures are supposed to be secret. We'd like to keep it that way.

-I can hold a secret, I tell him. No problem.

-Good.

The pilot stares up at the clouds with his helmet still on. He's dressed in a canvas jumper with the visor of the helmet obscuring most of his face.

-Looks like it might rain again later, he shouts at the medic.

-Always does, the medic replies.

The medic glances back at the empty gurney and around at the blinking red eyes on the hospital roof. We seem very small together beneath the fangs of large buildings. He is restless now that he's back on the ground. He doesn't like it this way. There is something seductive about hovering.

-Are you looking for anything particular at the hospital? the medic asks.

-I'm looking for Dot, I tell him.

-Oh Dot, yeah.

-You know where she is? I ask.

-You know where Dot is now? the medic shouts to the pilot.

-V Wing, the pilot replies, flicking his cigarette.

-Where's that? I ask.

-Don't know, says the medic. I don't know anything about what goes on down there. Or even how they organize things. We stay up on the roof, mostly. If we have a body, they take it with them into the freight elevator. If we need fuel, they funnel it up onto the roof.

He points to the hull of a closed mouth at the other end of the building. There is an airstream trailer set up beside it where I assume the pilot and the medic sleep. The pilot is back in the helicopter now, rummaging through the cargo panel.

-Should I try the elevator then? I ask.

-You could.

-It seems like the only way down.

The medic shrugs. The pilot removes a telescopic fishing rod from the helicopter and comes back onto the helipad with a tackle box. I watch for a moment as he fixes his lure. When it's clear the medic has no more advice, I start walking in the direction of the freight elevator. There is a small clothesline of canvas uniforms flapping in the wind beside the airstream trailer. I press the overlarge call button beside the elevator doors and wait.

Behind me, the pilot has extended the fishing rod to about 15 feet. It's clear he plans to cast into the bay. The reel on the rod is long and heavy and seems to hold miles of fishing line in its coil. As the elevator door opens, he fixes his shoulders. I step inside. The pilot pulls the long rod back in a thin and extended arch, pointing toward the lighthouse. The door slides shut again. I don't know where the elevator is going. The only button on the interior panel is a rectangular box reading *down*. I press it and wait.

It has been a long time since I visited Dot at St Killian's. I am not sure exactly how long it has been, but it has been some time. No one can remember when Dot wasn't sick, but before she was sick, she worked at St Killian's. At first, they tried to get her to leave the hospital, but she insisted she was more comfortable here. A handful of the nurses and doctors remember working with her during their residencies, but most don't. She still reads the occasional patient chart and does the occasional freelance work for people like Zed, but mostly she doesn't do anything anymore. They say she has Whittling's Disease. Or something very much like it.

The elevator opens into a long white corridor lined with hospital rooms. Crowds of doctors in white lab coats and nurses in green scrubs filter like clouds of neon between the enclaves. The doorways to the rooms are all open. Gray discarded clumps of medical equipment line the hall, and at the end of the corridor, there is a pair of double doors that seem to be receding. I step out of the elevator.

As I walk, the medical staff filters around me. The doctors follow the lead of brown wooden clipboards and the nurses carry bedpans and prepare lancets. Some wheel metal carts with probing instruments and jars of cotton balls and tongue depressors. In the hospital rooms, the beds are filled by shriveled patients, writhing in the grip of thin bedsheets. The doctors stand around them and take notes. The nurses record the readouts of tall blinking machines and whisper softly to one another. There are a lot of medical professionals in ———. Nearly six for every patient.

-Are you looking for something? one of the nurses asks me. He is a thin man with a shaved head wearing purple nitrile gloves.

-Where am I?

-You're on the radiology wing, he says. Are you looking for something?

-I'm looking for a friend, I tell him. She may be on V Wing

-No one uses that system anymore, the nurse blinks. Who's your friend?

-Her name is Dot. Do you know her?

-Not me, he says. But Dr Ruth knows her. Can you wait?

-Sure.

The nurse peels away from me and re-enters the cloud. I watch as he weaves through the hallway, but I lose his head the further he goes down. There is something vacant about the staffs' faces here. There are lines in their skin where there shouldn't be lines. Their eyes recede inside their heads. Their skin is sickly and pale. I think about renovations here. I think about the beds replaced by leg presses, pec decks, and seated curl machines. I think about the nurses' station replaced by blenders for protein shakes like at St Killian's South. There is a shroud of interchangeability to the buildings in ——. Like the rooms are only a foreclosure away from becoming something else. A missed payment on a balance sheet waiting to happen. Funeral parlors have become roller rinks here. Racetracks have become waste management plants that way. It is the same with people.

-You said you were looking for Dot? an older woman in a white overcoat asks me. Her hair is faded black with streaks of white running over her skull into a ponytail.

-Yes, do you know her?

-No, but Nurse Taylor might.

-Can you take me to him?

-Is it urgent? she asks. I'm sort of busy.

-I'd like to see her, I tell her. That's all.

Dr Ruth sighs. She chisels a line of scratches onto her clipboard then looks away. There are long wisps of black and gray hairs stuck to the lapels of her lab coat. She seems to have aged in place. The tendons in her neck forecast the shell she's becoming. The rest of the medical staff seem to be doing the same.

-I can take you down to Heart & Vascular, but you'll have to find him from there, she says at last.

-That's fine, I tell her. Thank you.

Without speaking, Dr Ruth turns and leads me through the corridor. Her legs make long extended sweeps as the rest of the medical staff congeal out of our way. I look for the bald nurse again but can't find him. The rooms tick past with separate lives twisting between their walls like silver bugs trapped beneath floorboards. The staff take notes to memorialize the decay.

Dr Ruth turns into a stairwell, and we walk down a flight of concrete steps. In the stairwell, Dr Ruth pauses. She twists a signet ring on her index finger. She wears a small, fragile St Christopher's medallion around her neck on a thin silver chain.

-I hope you don't think I'm rude, she tells me. I'm just very busy today.

-I understand, I say to her. It's ok.

-He's just through that door, she gestures. Just ask for him by name. They'll help you.

I nod and walk down the rest of the staircase. She holds onto the railing like someone sick at sea. Dr Ruth reminds me of my landlady, but probably only because they are both thin and older with spindly black hair. Dr Ruth recedes as I knock on the door to Heart & Vascular.

A few moments later, the door slides to a crack. The figure behind the door is small and mousy and dressed in a white lab coat over dark red scrubs.

-What are you looking for? she asks me.

-I'm looking for Nurse Taylor, I say.

-Is that all?

-Well. I'm really looking for Dot.

-I don't think Dot knows Nurse Taylor.

-What about the other way around?

-What other way?

-Does Nurse Taylor know Dot?

The mousy doctor furrows her eyebrows. Her face is very tan and she has her hair coiled together in frail braids. Her eyes are dark and she has a birthmark stretching the length of her right jaw. Her breathing is very heavy.

-Let me think about it, she says and turns back into the corridor.

The door slides shut again. Dr Ruth has left the staircase. It is only me now and the surrounding silence. The air in the stairs is hot and damp. I wonder what Lil is doing at this moment. I wonder if she is still awake. I wonder what time it is and if she's playing the drums or if she's crying and tearing down her fairy lights. It feels like it's very late now, but I have no way of knowing. There are not a lot of clocks in ———. There are not a lot of reasons to know what time it is either. The door to Heart & Vascular slides open again.

-This is Nurse Taylor, the mousy doctor says, gesturing to the man beside her in the doorway. He might be able to help.

-Hello.

-Hello, says Nurse Taylor.

Nurse Taylor is a middle-aged man with thinning yellow hair and a red drinker's nose. His gut hangs awkwardly into his scrubs and there seems to be a delay in how his senses process his surroundings. He holds on to the mousy doctor's elbow and looks at me like a relative he can't quite place.

-I'm looking for Dot, I tell him.

-Dot?

-Yes, do you know her?

-I remember, says Nurse Taylor vacantly, in a husky voice. I remember, I do.

The mousey doctor vanishes from off Nurse Taylor's shoulder as he stares into the air above my head. Behind him, I can see the flow of medical staff filtering through the hallway. The red and white fabrics seeping into each other like cardinals in the Holy See. Nurse Taylor begins shuffling away from the stairwell. I follow him out into the flow.

The Heart & Vascular wing is much like Radiology, only the staff has changed. Their uniforms have changed and there's a certain ruddiness to their complexions. A heaviness to the way they breathe. It feels hotter down here than on Radiology but only because everyone here seems to be sweating. I wonder how may floors there are at St Killian's. I wonder what they wear in the Maternity Ward. Or in Pediatrics.

-Do you know much about the other floors? I ask Nurse Taylor.

-Without desire, we live in hope, he tells me.

-Oh.

When we get to the nurse's station, there's a small clot of staff huddled around. They turn to Nurse Taylor and stare at him for a moment. The corridor seems to fall silent as he approaches the desk.

-He's looking for Dot, I can hear one of the nurses whisper.

-I heard he came from the roof, another says.

Nurse Taylor pushes past them and picks up the plastic desk phone and puts it to his ear. His graying eyebrows furrow. He appears to be listening to someone speaking on the other end.

-Yes, he says. Yes, Yes. Very well then. I'll tell him.

-Tell me what? I ask

He hangs up the phone. By now, most of the nurses have dissipated. The few that remain seem distracted by open folders and small tasks.

-She's in the trauma unit, Nurse Taylor says.

-Are you sure?

-An ill way thou goest.

-I'm just trying to end up in the right place, I tell him.

He grunts and shuffles away. I start following him again. For some reason, I'm worried what happens if they throw me off the floor. I'm worried what happens if they x-ray my chest and find I have heart palpitations. I'd never felt it before, but St Killian's is not a place where I want to get lost. Or trapped inside. I can understand now why Ms Tupelo never wanted to go.

We get a little further down the side hallway and Nurse

Taylor suddenly stops. His watery eyes tilt upwards to the fluorescent tubes in the ceiling, and he lifts his hand to cross himself. His lips move silently against one another like fish at play. When he is finished, he turns to a panel in the wall and pulls a silver handle open. The panel reveals a dumbwaiter that has been tucked behind the panel's frame.

-Get in, he says.

-Is this the only way down?

-No, there are other ways.

-Is this way the quickest?

-Not particularly, he tells me. But it is a way.

-Will they tell me where she is when I get down there?

-No, you'll have to find her for yourself. They're very busy down there, he explains.

-Will they know I'm coming?

-They should.

I nod and climb into the dark box and suck my knees into my chest. Nurse Taylor gives a small nod and closes the panel behind me again. I can feel my breath swirling inside the blackness now. For a moment, I imagine the cable snapping. I imagine this in elevators all the time, but somehow it seems worse now in the darkness and with my knees sucked into my chest. I wonder for a moment if this is how babies feel just before they are born. I can almost hear the sounds Mr Kim makes. The grinding of pumice across callouses. Floss moving between teeth. I wonder why he stays in there. I wonder why he rides between the floors without stopping. Now the freight elevator begins its descent.

When the dumbwaiter stops, the door to the trauma unit slides automatically open. The uniforms here are a deep purple and the staff seem to be moving slower here than on other floors. I expect the sound of screaming, but there is none. I emerge from the dumbwaiter, unfolding myself outward into the hall.

The nurses and doctors try not to look at me, and again I wonder how thin I look. I wonder about the clothes I'm wearing.

It seems sad to worry about this kind of thing, but people assume it's something you're in control of. The arrangement of the hospital wings has begun making sense now. The way the floors are set up. I move down the hallway past the patient rooms toward the set of swinging double doors.

As I'm about halfway down, something causes me to stop. Someone I've seen before. In one of the hospital beds, the man whose eyes Ng thumbed out is talking to a nurse. The nurse is being patient with what the man is saying, but it's clear he is very bored. The nurses on this floor have swollen irises and hold their own fingers together a lot. After a while, the nurse begins backing slowly out of the room as the blind man keeps talking.

-You know him? the nurse whispers to me when he reaches the doorway.

-He used to play tennis, I think.

-He told me it was golf.

-Did he tell you how he lost his eyes?

-He says it was a welding accident.

-Do you believe him?

-No. I know it's a lie, but it doesn't make any difference now that he's here.

-Do you want to know how it actually happened?

-Not really, no.

The nurse sighs and walks off into the next room. I keep moving down the hall. The blind man continues talking into the empty room as I pass his window. I wonder absently about the story he's telling. The story that doesn't exist or might exist and how the holes in his head might be the only thing concretely real about him. I think about the driver in the ice cream truck also. About the story he's telling some hapless passenger crossing town in the middle of the night. About false wounds in Dabiq bleeding out like imaginary women who all respect power or men with something stupid to say. I think there are a lot of stories like this in ——. Stories people tell themselves and tell others about themselves and how they got to be this way. Stories we tell just to get along. I think the nurse is probably right. It doesn't matter. None of it does. Truth is something we reveal to one another in passing, glancing blows. It's what we say about the clouds. About the weather. About the rain.

At the end of the hall there's a large mahogany door leading into the last room. For some reason, it seems like the door belongs to Dot. I knock on the wood and step away.

12.

When Dot opens the door, it takes her a while to remember my name. She's stands crumpled in the doorway, strapped standing into a vertical mobility machine. She wears a blue jean jacket and a white motorcycle scarf over her hospital gown with black leather fingerless gloves on either hand. There's a pair of bronze-colored racing goggles obscuring half her face.

-Oh, Y, she says. This is embarrassing.

-What's embarrassing?

-Just come in. I was just playing make-believe, she tells me.

-That's ok.

The mobility machine wheels away from the door at a crooked angle, swiping backward and bumping into a *chabudai* Dot has set up in the corner. A set of teacups rattle aggressively.

-Fucking thing sucks, Dot curses.

-Do you need help? I ask.

-*No.*

She pushes the machine forward again and knocks against a bedpost. She then sweeps the whole apparatus in a semicircle and comes to rest in the center of the room. She lifts a wavering hand and slides the goggles off her face, grimacing.

-I don't know why I keep that fucking thing around, she says. I used to know how to do the whole ceremony, but I'm gradually forgetting. It's a lot about touch and the way you hold things. The *temae.* These are the things I'm forgetting. Subtle sensory knowledge. It's not like state capitals or structures of the sacrum, you know?

-It's ok.

Dot sighs. Her room is well furnished. There is red carpeting and warm lighting and a set of appliances whose names I don't recall. It is a different type of non-remembering than what Dot is talking about, but the wood cabinetry, the foot stools, the credenza. They don't register. A queen-sized bed dominates the center of the room as the rest of the furniture emanates out around it, taking up territory in different quadrants and corners. The bed has been tightly made. There is a large harp standing beside a vanity table.

-What brings you here? Dot asks me.

-I was with Zeb earlier.

-Oh. Do you want an egg?

-If you have them.

-I only have deviled duck eggs, really. I'm not sure if that'll work.

-Who makes those kinds of rules anyway, I shrug.

-Check the refrigerator then.

Dot gestures with her eyes to a set of cabinets that look like they might house a television set. Then she turns the mobility machine over toward the window. I take off my shoes and cross the red carpeting, kneeling in front of the cabinet, fiddling with the ornate key. She extends a grabber stick from the machine and uses it to pull back the heavy velvet curtains.

Dot's small refrigerator houses an odd assortment of cans and jars. Noticeably, there is an Spruce Cobra trapped inside a bottle of rice wine. Different types of foie gras. A clear plastic container of shark's fin soup. I see what looks like a Tupperware container full of green eggs and pull it out from the clutter.

-I thought you said they were deviled.

-Oh. That's just my word for it, Dot says. It's balut.

-What's balut?

-Fertilized duck egg. They steam it with the embryo still inside.

-Christ.

Dot doesn't say anything. She's staring out at the black swamp of the harbor. In the distance, there's a blinking white light. I put the eggs back in the refrigerator. Somehow it feels like the cleansing ritual with it wouldn't work or wouldn't come out right.

-A lot of people like cruelty-free food, Dot smirks. Not me.

-Cruelty heavy? I ask.

-You know, there's a theory in certain parts of the world that an animal tastes better if it's suffered while being slaughtered. There are certain death hormones that have an inimitable taste.

-You care about taste?

-Not really.

There are stacks of scans scattered on Dot's desk. Some are printouts from MRI machines. Others are simple pictures of body parts people send her. She keeps them all in folders beside her fax machine and marks them up with red wax pen.

-You know, there's a way of eating monkey's brain where they crack the skull open with a hammer. You eat the brain while the monkey is still alive.

-I didn't know that.

-They say that's how people contracted Creutzfeldt–Jakob disease.

-What's that?

-It's prion disease. It sends protein chains through your neural tissue. Eventually you become someone else. Then you forget how to breathe. Then you die.

-Huh.

Dot turns away from the window and gestures to the bed with her eyes again. It takes me a minute to realize what she's suggesting before I go over and take a seat. She wheels the machine beside me and angles it so the forks at the base slide under the bed. She lifts the motorcycle scarf up with her shaking hand and slides it between her teeth. Then she taps a button with her thumb.

The mobility machine folds itself downward, and Dot screams. Her teeth sink through the white fabric and the chords of her neck strain. Tears burst from her eyelids as her body shakes. The scream continues, muffled by the motorcycle scarf.

She ends up on the bed beside me in a seated position, still radiating pain. It takes her a while to become steady again.

Whittling's disease attacks the joints. It makes movement nearly impossible. It is a cruel and exacting disease. St Killian is supposedly the patron saint of rheumatism. The tears begin drying on Dot's face. It is a horrible thing to get used to the feeling of tears drying on one's face.

-How's Zed doing? she asks at last.

-He's ok.

-He kill anyone tonight?

-Yes.

-Is that why you're here?

-That's what got me here, yes. But I was coming anyway.

-What were you coming for?

-El went over Jersey.

-Oh, Dot says.

-Were you close?

-No, not really. No.

-That's ok. I've been hearing that a lot tonight.

Dot takes a deep breath. She breathes in through her nose and lets the breath distill through her body. I wonder what medications they have her on to manage the pain. I don't see any pills around, but I imagine the situation is as much under control as she can take.

-I'm sorry I was curt with you earlier. It's been a rough couple of days.

-I understand that.

-You're not into animals, are you?

-No really. No.

She stares off into the wall. I see our bodies reflected in the vanity mirror and am afraid I look thin again. Dot has long wavy brown hair and a small, pale face. She used to be a renowned general practitioner, I think. That's why they let her stay in the hospital. There are plaques on her wall with the obscure names of bequeathed foundations listed above some kind of prize. It used to take them ten minutes to give Dot an introduction before she spoke. She used to be quite the institution around here. Before the disease took that away.

-How have you been? Dot asks.

-I've been alright.

-I think that's probably what you always say.

-Doesn't everyone.

-Yes, it's very annoying. It's like we force it from one another. Alright-ness. You never realize how much of a practice it is until 'alright' becomes an even bigger lie.

-It's polite, I think.

-Yes. Polite.

We fall silent. I look for the fishing line outside in the harbor but can't see anything in the night. It has started to rain. The curtains on Dot's window are only pulled halfway closed. I think of the dead man out in the harbor and about the lost cars of the abandoned subway trains. I think it's nice the hospital faces the water. It feels right this way. I look at Dot, and she seems to be getting embarrassed. Her face twitches and her cheeks are flushed. She kneads her lips together and bites the inside of her mouth.

-Can I ask you something, Y?

-Sure.

-But can I ask you to do something?

-Absolutely.

-I wouldn't normally ask but well. You've never been one for small talk and it's something I really need.

-You can ask.

-Can you...she trails off, kneading her lips again. Can you... Can you touch me?

-Sure, Dot, I whisper.

I reach my hand out for her arm where it's leveled in the air by the mobility machine. Her body looks thin beneath the thick fabric of her jean jacket. I can see the bend where her elbow curves away from me.

-No, she says sharply. Can you *touch* me, can you…can you touch my breast? Can you touch my areola?

She tilts her head away slightly and endures another ripple of pain. Her shoulders react to the pain in her neck, and there's a chain reaction of muscles chaffing against tendons beneath her skin. A fresh tear leaks from her eye.

-I hate to ask, I hate asking. I've always hated asking, I just.

-It's ok. Really. It's ok.

-I know with the curse and all you can't do certain things, but…

-Really. It's ok.

I unwind the scarf slowly from around her neck. My fingers brush the soft flesh beneath her jaw, and she trembles. I lift the scarf over her head and fold it softly onto the mattress like the shed skin of a snake. There's a special zipper sewn onto the back of Dot's jean jacket so that it can be split in the back and then slid off her arms so that she can remain inside the mobility frame. I pull the zipper down gently, letting it skip over the knots of her vertebrae. I peel the fabric forward as it sloughs off her thin shoulders and hold it in the air so it can slip down her forearms. I undo the buckling on her gloves. There is some pain as her fingers come together so that the leather can come off them before I take the halves of the jacket away.

Dot sits now with her arms bare in her white hospital gown. The material is thin and diaphanous and I can see the shape of her thin body in the glow of the warm light. Her eyes are closed and she is measuring her breathing. I reach to untie the string and pull apart the knot to let the dress fall down her shoulders. Dot shudders again. I try moving closer to her on the bed in a way that won't slip her into the fissure my weight leaves on the mattress. I place one hand on the other side of her body and slide the other over her sternum.

-Gently, she whispers. I'm sorry, gently.

-Ok.

I move the pressure off my palm and reach down into the fabric of her gown. There is a certain utility in this. Like surgery or autopsy. My hand finds the small bulb of her breast, and I think of the Palimistrist and what she said about my palms. I hope Dot doesn't mind. The outturned dial of her nipple fits into the slot between my fingers. I think about the lockpicks in the pocket of the dead man. I wonder what he'd have to say about intimacy. I wonder if that helicopter had stayed in the air forever and if that bullet hole hadn't killed him, if I would have ever asked. Dot sighs. Her breath shakes as it echoes from her body. I keep palpating Dot's nipple with my thumb. Our heads are very close together now. My mouth sits just beside her ear. She inhales again.

-The scarf, she pants as her chest shakes.

-What?

-No, don't stop. The scarf. The scarf.

Dot's jaw opens, and her eyes shut. I grasp what it is she's saying and pick up the white fabric from her bed. I slide it back into her mouth. My hand keeps moving, but it feels suddenly far away. Cut off from the main circuitry. Disembodied, like departing trains. Dot comes. She hits the stand-up button on her machine and it drags her upright as my hand slips over her shoulder. She screams into the scarf and shakes and moans. The strength leaves her legs, but the machine keeps her vertical. Aftershocks of pain and orgasm trade in swells through her body like the echoing of waves. It is a while before her breathing dies back down again.

-Thank you, she says, spitting out her scarf.

-It's no problem.

-I haven't been touched in so long.

-It's no problem at all.

She wheels over to the window and stares out again at the bay. The bright light at the center of the harbor continues its sweep over the hospital. The moon hangs high with a closed face.

-He knew El, Dot says softly.

-Who did?

-Him. Nat. In the lighthouse.

-Did he?

-I'm pretty sure.

-I didn't know El went to the lighthouse.

-El went a lot of strange places.

-Huh.

-You don't believe me?

-I've seen a lot of people tonight, that's all.

-Lucky you.

Dot has her face turned away so I can't see if she's crying. I slipped the scarf crookedly over her shoulder and now the weight of the spent saliva where the fabric bent in her mouth is dragging the fabric down her chest. I stand up and move to the window and take the scarf away. I pull the gown back up over Dot's shoulder and retie the knot behind her spine.

-You don't even have this, do you? she asks.

-What do you mean?

-With the curse and all. You couldn't do this.

-No. That'd give me another ghost.

-You wouldn't want that.

-Of course not.

-Why? What are they to you?

-It's complicated.

-I'm surprised you haven't dug the world a cemetery by

now. I know I would have.

-You wouldn't, I tell her. You think you would, but you wouldn't. It's different when they're there at night. Staring you in the face.

-Is that the only reason?

I stand beside her and put my palms down on the long metal windowsill. I see my face for a moment, reflected in the glass. The black water in the harbor fills in the features of my skin, and I see my whole being trapped between the room, the water, and the windowpane.

-The supposed worth of a stranger's life is the only thing keeping me moving, I say. The people I've hurt serve a reminder to myself of why I'm still alive. If they're worth nothing. If their pain and their death is worth nothing. Then everything is. I have to believe in their significance to believe in my own. Without it, I would probably just end up over Jersey.

-Is that why you're looking for El then? To make sure that he has a witness?

-Yes. I think that's why. It's not that I'm a good person it's just that…

-It's just what?

-Every life means everything.

-I see.

Dot wheels away from the window and uses the extendable grabber claw on her machine to open a drawer on her desk.

-You know, if they hadn't taken away my prescription pad, I could have done something for you, she says.

-It's alright, really.

-I don't like to be in debt, Dot says harshly. So if you reach in there, you'll find a scroll.

-What's on it?

-I don't really know. But when I was still practicing, people would come in with all types of ailments. Most you could cure with good diet. Some requiring surgery. Others would just need time to resolve. But some. Our medicine had no control over. Do you follow me?

-Yes.

-Take it then. I may want it back at some point, but I haven't used it in years. Take it.

I go over to the open cabinet and take out the small coil of paper Dot gestures toward. I slide it into the silver case it belongs to and put the case into my pocket.

-Go see Nat now, she tells me.

-Do you know the way out of here?

-Through the hospital?

-Yeah.

-I used to. Not anymore. They change the wings around periodically. Their places and their names. I'm honestly surprised you found me.

-How do I get down then?

-You can use the trash chute, she says, wheeling back over to the window.

Dot uses her grabber to open the curtain all the way, revealing a long orange tube sealed into the glass. There's a sliding plastic grate over the entrance, but it looks big enough to crawl inside.

-Is it safe? I ask.

-This time of night, they haven't emptied the trash yet. Most of it is medical supplies. Cardboard and maternity gowns.

-No needles or anything? Nothing hard?

-They wouldn't throw away needles in a dumpster.

-I'm not sure.

-Come on. Haven't you always wanted to do this? People have done it before. They've been ok.

-If you say so.

I pick up my shoes from the corner and cross over the room. I slide them on as Dot pulls back the grate.

-Slow yourself down as much as you can before you hit the bottom. Use your feet and jacket so your palms don't chafe.

-Might do me some good.

I climb feet first into the tube and feel the ground drop out beneath my legs. I hold myself up for a moment with my arms and stare up at Dot. She looks like a Madonna encircled by the orange of the trash chute.

-See you later, Dot, I say.

-See you later, Y. Thank you for coming. There will still be some men down by the harbor if you need a ride.

-Ok.

I pull my hands into my chest and drop.

14.

Dot was right. When I reach the bottom, I land in a clump of hospital masks and old rubber mattresses. I look up at Dot's window but see the curtains have been pulled shut. I lift myself up out of the dumpster and grab ahold of the metal siding. In the parking lot, there is a procession of nurses dragging carts full of computer processors.

-Are you getting rid of those now? I ask them, jumping down onto the ground again.

-Yes, says one of the nurses in blue scrubs. It's time for them to go.

-Huh.

The nurses begin heaving the CPUs into the dumpster. The metal clashing against itself makes a sound like the banging of a cracked church bell. I walk away from the hospital down toward the water. There is a cluster of nurses in black scrubs milling around in the flower garden. They have long shears out and are cutting different shapes in the hedge displays. A few of them stand on long rickety stepladders. Others sit on plastic coolers and cut their fingernails.

-What do you think? one asks as I pass the gardenias.

-Are those still in season?

He shrugs and walks away. I think they must be the morticians. The hospital makes them come out here twice a day to be around life again. It helps keep them sane so that they don't burn out so often.

The promenade for the harbor opens up immediately from the hospital. The Old Docks are a short walk along the waterfront in the dead middle, where the bend of the water presses inward on the City. There have been various different efforts to improve the promenade over the years. Sometimes they add a pier. Sometimes they take one away. —— is unsure of what to do with itself at its edges. The structures of the City foment inwardly in confusion. At one point, people suggested just filling the harbor in completely, getting rid of the water and building a wall facing the bay. It's been a lingering ballot initiative ever since.

The Old Docks are only used now for private vessels. Decorative schooners and fishing boats. There are a few houseboats down there too and a few boat motels. The ferrymen have their own separate dock and go out each morning to shuffle rides back and forth to different corners of the bay. The teeth of the marina jut out into the water. I wait a while before entering. I listen to the sound of the water lapping against wood in the dark. I think about the dead man again and if the ripple of his death had managed to get to the shoreline. Somehow in the ocean, I imagine every disruption is recorded. A minor alteration to the pattern of the waves. Or else the moon wipes everything clean. That's possible too.

A woman brushes past me with an armful of groceries. She's tall and very thin and moving in the direction of one of the boat motels. A man watches her from the upper deck with a toothbrush in his mouth. Another girl sits on the lower banister, reading from an old magazine with faded pages. There are houseboat dormitories too. It's a cheap way to live downtown. I think Wu used to live in one of those before he ate the colander of gravel. I think about asking the tall woman if she knew Wu as she waits for the man with the toothbrush to lower the drawbridge. A long stalk of celery sticks out the top of her bag. I think about asking, but I'm afraid of explaining why I'm asking and have her supply me with another name. Most people seem to know someone who's gone over, and they'll usually tell you how. I walk off in the direction of the ferrymen.

On the ferrymen's dock, the remaining workers are engaged in a combat ritual. A circle of ferrymen surrounds a single dancer who is cartwheeling and jabbing at the air with his feet.

The ferrymen in the circle stand very still and silent, except for the few who are playing instruments. The collision of the dancing man's hands on the docks creates a gentle creak. When the man tires himself out, he rejoins the circle and another man takes up the beat. I approach the edge of the circle where one of the outlying ferrymen notices me.

-Going somewhere? he asks.

-Yes, I'm trying to see Nat.

-Tonight?

-Yeah.

The ferryman turns and whispers into another ferryman's ear. The message begins making its way around the circle, emanating outward in either direction as the ferrymen take turns placing it in one another's skulls. Eventually, the instrumentalists stop playing. The dancer in the center does a few more handstands and then stops also.

-What gives? he asks.

-Man says he wants to see Nat tonight, one of the ferrymen in the circle says.

-Tonight? asks the dancer.

-Yeah, another one says.

The circle splits open. All of the ferrymen are dressed in heavy black fishing jackets and have scars on their faces and hands. There are a few gas lanterns lit on the pier, but mostly there is only darkness and shadows. Their boats are all tied up in a long convoy beside the docks. The ferrymen form in a V shape now, all staring inwards at me.

-You're the one who wants to see Nat? the dancing man asks.

-Yes.

-Tonight?

-Yes.

The ferrymen all look down at their boots and shuffle back and forth. I feel bad for having disrupted their game, but there is no other way across the water. It can't be helped.

-It's for a friend, I tell them. One of Nat's friends went over Jersey.

-Oh, the ferrymen say in muddled unison.

-I'll take you then, one volunteer steps forward.

-If not him, then me, says another.

It seems like the other ferrymen all plan on volunteering, but they're content to let the ones who stepped forward serve as emissaries. Of all the people in ——, it is assumed that the ferrymen take Jersey the most seriously. Something about being so close with the harbor and the symbolic role they play. The Charon Society has a pancake breakfast to raise money for public coffins every year and to mend the nets that are used to dredge the harbor. I've never been. I've heard it's ok.

-You then, I say to the first man who stepped forward.

-Right this way.

I follow him down the dock as the circle of ferrymen reforms. The beat struck by the instruments kicks up again. Another ferryman returns to the middle to keep dancing.

-Why do they do it? I ask the guide I'm with as we climb into his boat.

-It's called Engolo, he says. It's a combat dance invoking the spirit world. Notice how much time we spend on our hands. That's how the spirits walk. Upside-down.

-On their hands like that?

-Yes. Everything is inverted.

-Huh.

The ferryman unties the knot tethering us to the dock. He pushes the motorboat sideways into the water and wraps his hand around the steering lever. He punches the carburetor and twists the throttle. The motor starts. Water churns behind us as the boat steers out into the bay. I sit in the small padded seat before the bow and wrap my arms together. It's colder now than it had been before.

The ferryman is old, I think. He's got a mangled face and

greasy black hair that slides off the back of his head. In another place, he might look like a barfly. His voice is low and gravely and he speaks like he's hiding marbles in his jaw.

-You see the man come off the helicopter earlier? I ask.

-Yes.

-Did you retrieve him?

-Not me personally, but we did.

-What happens then?

-Roll them up in a carpet, usually. Put them on a truck.

-Where does the truck go?

-We don't know. We don't ask. It's better if the psychopomps don't communicate.

-One long impenetrable chain.

-Something like that.

The City rises up behind us. The long, wide face of St Killian's watches over the bay. I think about the bodies emanating into ——'s bloodstream. I think about the dead man's wet and lifeless body in the back of an ice cream truck, covered up by Klondike Bars and Push Pops. I think of El's body being shipped around —— like that too. It is important that the process is dispersed. That no one takes on too great a role. The City survives itself this way. A fine mist of water flies over the boat as we chop through the current. The light from the lighthouse skims across the water.

-Not much to look at, is it? the ferryman asks.

-You mean the City?

-Yeah.

-I suppose it's not.

-My father worked at the computer plant here.

-A lot of people say that now.

-It's true.

-A lot of people say that also.

-I don't think you're a tourist, the ferryman tells me. I don't expect you to tip. A tourist wouldn't be trying to see Nat this late anyway. I just want to let you know what kind of man I am.

-I appreciate that, I say.

The ferryman nods. The lighthouse seems to be receding into the distance as we skim closer over the harbor. Its spire sticks out in the darkness like a cigarette shoved face down in a succulent. Like an incense stick abandoned in a gym locker. The white sweep of its lantern blitzes the sky. For a moment, I think of drowning.

-It looks like rain, the ferryman says.

-Always does, I say.

-No, the ferryman shakes his head, fumbling with a hatch over the ballast. I don't mean it like how you mean it.

-How do you mean it?

A bolt of lightning splits the sky, crossing over the backside of the lighthouse like a seam being ripped apart. From out over the ocean, a curtain of clouds seems to be closing in. The lighthouse shines an infrequent light on the billowing mass of black weather fast approaching the dinghy.

-Take this, the ferryman says, handing me a tangle of dark green canvas. Wrap yourself in it.

-What will we do if it knocks over the ship?

-We'll cross that bridge when we get to it.

I tuck myself into the fetal position beneath the curve of the gunwale beside the center thwart. The ferryman pulls his hat over his face and twists down on the throttle. The hull of the ship slams against the water. Another string of lightning rips out. I think of how I'm already wrapped in canvas. In case they need to call me a truck.

The rain hits all at once. Like a payload of white phosphorous. The ferryman bears down on the throttle as we're knocked back by the crashing of waves. I look out to see the lighthouse swallowed by the storm, the pillar of light fighting with the clouds to escape into the swirling firmament. The ferryman shouts but his words are obscured by the rattle of thunder.

On the other side, —— is equally consumed by the squall. The fangs downtown have been blotched out, their yellow eyes smothered. The hatch on the ballast flaps open again like a jaw that's been split. The ferryman slams his boot on it, bracing against the rain with his free hand. On the crest of the swells, the motor skips out of the water and slaps impotently at the churning bay, letting off a tortured whirring sound into the storm. The ferryman is shouting something again. I look out directly at the anvil shade of darkness closing over us.

The clouds ignite. The lightning pops and shoots through the sky like the branches of a dead tree. Prairiefire Crabapple. The ferryman pitches forward. He drops over the center thwart and begins spasming like a fish. The throttle of the motor tips backwards. I slam into the gunwale as the dinghy starts to spiral. My hand shoots out into the darkness. The ferryman's twitching body rolls over me. Like the body of a man brained with a folding chair. I launch myself forward and pull the motor back up, steering the ship into the wake again. Vomit slams against my teeth. I clamp my feet over the ferryman's chest to keep him from capsizing the vessel and ending up another twitching corpse beneath ——'s harbor.

As I strain, two limbs over the ferryman's body, one hand on the stern seat, one hand on the throttle, drenched in rain, I'm reminded of the Hecatoncheire. Maybe that's what Tess and Bell are missing. They should tie the artists' hips together and drop them into a sideless glass water tank. In rats, this is called the despair test. Scientists use it to test the efficacy of antidepressants. The time the rat spends immobile, accepting its fate, is used as a metric. The longer the rat spends actively fighting, the more effective the antidepressant is deemed to be. A lot of medication gets approved that way. It seems at last as if the lighthouse is drawing closer. The ferryman's limbs continue whipping against the hull of the dinghy. I grit my teeth.

Finally, I can see the actual body of the lighthouse come up over the bow. I am not sure where the shoreline will be. I am prepared to shred the motor by crashing it directly onto the bank. The squall has given us no choice. It is still uncomfortable to wait. It is uncomfortable to be crashing in the direction of something, knowing it is almost there, and still having to wait. In the clarity of spent adrenaline, I realize it is a familiar feeling. First the bow slides up the bank. Then the motor snags and yowls in the night, smothered by rock and sand. We come to a halt.

I fall out of the boat and drag the ferryman with me. The lapping surf bites my ankles as the ferryman's body continues to shake. I see a patch of grass upward from the beach and make for it, dragging us both through the sand. The ferryman drops behind me. I roll onto my back into the grass. I think about how turkeys are said to die from drowning in the rain with their mouths open. I think it's a beautiful way to go over, but I don't know of anyone who's tried it yet. I'm breathing heavy. The rain goes up my nose. The heavy iron door on the lighthouse swings open.

-Christ on a cracker! I hear Nat screaming, his footsteps closing in above my scalp.

-Him! Him! I point, moaning, still on my back.

Nat rushes past me, clutching an umbrella to his chest. When he gets to the beach, the umbrella immediately breaks back on itself, inverting into a funnel. How umbrellas must look in the spirit world. He snaps it back into position against the wind and crouches over the ferryman's twitching body. He sees the shipwrecked dinghy as it's swallowed back by the sea. Out behind the lighthouse, the squall seems to be breaking.

When the man is done twitching, Nat lifts him up and puts him on his side. The man exhales a phlegm of bile and seawater, snot mingling with his beard. Nat rubs the ferryman's back. I begin to feel my limbs again and push myself up onto my elbows. My head feels light. The two figures on the beach look like marionettes in a street performance. The way Nat moves like his arms are being jerked by unseen strings hanging far above him. When the ferryman is settled, Nat starts walking back toward me.

-What the hell were you doing out there? This time of night?

-Coming to see you, I tell him.

-Me?

-Yeah.

-Well, Nat trails off. You shouldn't have.

-Too late now.

Nat nods. He sticks out his hand to pull me up to my feet and starts dusting some of the sand off me. I hardly feel his hands as they touch fabric that's hardly mine. The rain has thinned to a drizzle. The ferryman is still stuck on the beach. Nat and I walk together down toward him again.

When we reach the beach, Nat stoops and uses the ferryman's hat to wipe the spit-up from his face and beard. He lets the spent fabric fall deflated back on the beach as the ferryman rocks back and forth on his side.

-My wife used to do that for me, he says.

-I think you had a seizure, says Nat.

-The lightning, I add.

The ferryman nods. Together we pull him up to standing. His legs won't support him and so we slide him back into a sit. Nat reaches his hand into the ferryman's jacket and starts undoing a strap tied to his pectoral. I think there might be bruising and blood on the ferryman's head, but in the darkness, it looks only like splotches of shadow. The rain has died down again.

-They all have one of these, Nat says, pulling something red and plastic from the ferryman's pocket.

-What is it? I ask.

-Flare gun.

-A signal?

-Yep.

Nat lifts the pistol over his head and fires it up into the darkness. The red light shoots out over the harbor, and in the distance, I can see the City again. The glowing orb makes an arch over the water then vanishes through the teeth of the City when it drops back into the waves. —— doesn't look so far away anymore. After a moment, we see another orb glide above the harbor in the distance. Then drop. Then fade.

-They're on their way, Nat says.

-The ferrymen?

-Yeah. They probably saw the squall also. And assumed.

-Do all the ferryman have epilepsy? I ask.

-They all have something, I'm afraid.

Nat folds the gun open and lets the empty cartridge fall out onto the beach. He hands the plastic back to the soaked ferryman. The ferryman slides it into the holster on his pectoral and looks away.

-I'm ashamed, he says softly.

-It happens, I say.

-Do you want to come in for coffee? Nat asks.

The fisherman hauls himself to his feet and shakes his head.

-No, I'll just wait for them down here on the beach.

-Ok.

Nat and I turn to walk back to the lighthouse. The ferryman puts his hands on his hips and stares out at the darkness of the bay.

15.

Inside the lighthouse, a long iron staircase curls up the interior like the elongated corpse of a fire escape. Nat has paved the ground floor with glossy wood paneling. A ballet barre swims in a ring. The walls, at least up to head level, are coated in mirror. Above that, exposed brick.

-Take your shoes off please, Nat asks.

-How do you keep all this clean?

-With enormous effort.

Nat hands me a pair of guest slippers. I take off my socks and slide the slippers over my feet. In the dryness of the lighthouse, I can feel how wet my clothes are. I feel bad to be dripping harbor water all over Nat's studio, but he doesn't seem to care. He pulls down an iron ladder connecting to the staircase, hanging above the ballet floor.

-We'll go upstairs and get dry, he says. Do you want something to eat?

-Do I look thin? I ask him.

Nat stares at me from above on the staircase and shakes his head. He's skilled with this type of question. Nat used to be a dancer before contracting a viral infectious disease. He lost three of the toes on his right foot to gangrene. Now he dances an odd and circuitous cripple's ballet. A bit like the whirling dervishes the Sufis make in meditation. Abandoning the nafs. He doesn't really dance while anyone is around though. I wonder if after she realized she'd be stuck in the underworld, Persephone kept eating pomegranate seeds. I haul myself up the ladder. Nat grips the banister as we climb the spiral up toward the wooden peak of the wooden ceiling.

At the end of the staircase, Nat opens a hatch and we pull ourselves up into his sitting room. The furniture is sparse and bare, but Nat keeps a collection of spinning plates, metronomes, and pendulum clocks lining the open space. A bit like chokies or totems. There is a curved infinity couch crutched beneath a porthole window. A wooden table with four wooden chairs. An electric tea kettle. A liquor shelf. A collection of tin dishware and cutlery. Some cabinets. A lamp. A sink.

-I can dry those on the stove upstairs if you like, Nat says, pointing to my clothes.

-Thank you, I tell him.

I take my coat off and empty my pockets onto the table. My cell phone and my radio are both soaked through and broken. It is a strange thing to see broken electronics. It is strange to own objects so capable of death and typically I try to avoid them. I still have the dead man's note, Peanut's bottle, Dot's scroll, and the Politician's campaign pin. They all seem much harder to kill. I suppose that is upsetting in its own right. Nat comes back with a heavy terrycloth robe as I slide off my wet clothing. It still feels like nothing lost, and even in the bareness of the air, I still feel insulated. The robe only helps me feel my own ribcage, the pressure of my bones wedged up tight against my skin.

When Nat comes back into the light, I get a clean look at him. He is dressed in black tights that bulge against his musculature like tightly stuffed trash bags. Everything but the depleted right leg that hangs off his body like an afterthought. His hair is clipped very close to his skull, making his forehead look very big. Like his brains are about to explode out of his ears.

-What brings you out here, Y?

-El's gone over Jersey, I tell him.

-Oh. I'm sorry to hear that, he says.

-Were you close?

-No, not really.

-I thought so. Dot told me you were is all.

-He came out here once or twice, I think. I can't quite remember. It could have been someone else. I'm not sure how Dot knows.

-The lighthouse means a lot to her, I think.

-Yeah.

We sit down in chairs together and stare at the floor. I can tell Nat is thinking about Jersey as he glances up at the dark porthole. Occasionally, the porthole glows white when the lighthouse beacon makes its pass overhead. They're chanting the Names of God on the radio now. I'm not sure this is a program Nat listens to. I'd like to listen for a little bit, but my radio has been fully shredded by the storm and Nat doesn't seem to have one out.

-Have you been listening to the radio tonight? I ask him.

-No. The signal is not very clear out here. I get some shortwave from the hospital, that's all.

-Oh.

-A man came off a helicopter tonight, Nat tells me.

-I know, I say. I was there.

-On the docks?

-No, in the helicopter.

-In the helicopter?

-Yes. I was going to see Dot.

-I didn't see him fall, Nat says. It was too dark.

-It was not an important failure, I say.

-I guess not.

Nat takes up his healthy foot and begins massaging it. He cracks the toes and inspects the callouses. He works his ankle into tight circles and runs his thumb over his metatarsal veins. He takes out a small green stone and rubs it against the center of his sole.

-This is the heart chakra, he says.

-I see.

He kneads the stone deep into his flesh. It looks like it might be jade or malachite. Nat knows a lot about minerals and about the body.

-I'm wondering if Dot didn't send you out here for another

reason.

-That could be the case.

-She used to be a doctor, you know.

-I know.

-Someone who always seems to be trying to take diseases from other people.

-Yes.

-Did you hear the one about the doctor who went to see the clown about her cyclothymia?

-Why would she talk to a clown about that?

-I don't know, Nat sighs. Everyone has got to talk to somebody, I guess.

Nat puts the stone back in his pocket and places his foot on the floor, flexing his toes. His pupils have expanded in the lowlight into obsidian holes. I think about offering him the scroll, but I assume he can see it on the desk. I pull it out of its silver canister and hand it to him anyway.

-What's this?

-Dot gave it to me. She said it might help.

Nat opens it and holds it open over his knee. It takes a while for him to fiddle with the paper. His eyebrows crease in concentration. He walks over to the lamp and holds it up to the light. I can see the parchment illuminated and the ink detailed into the gossamer page. The writing is very thin and very small, and there seem to be diagrams and illustrations drawn on some of the paper.

-I don't think I can help you with this, he says.

-Do you know what it is?

-It's a codex of some kind. Something ancient, maybe. I'm not sure why Dot would have it or why she would give it to you. Again, she seems prone to this kind of thing.

-Well. Thanks anyway.

Nat hands it back to me, and I slide it into its silver case. The scroll seems to have annoyed him. Nat rubs his thumb against his bottom lip.

-I don't think that was it, Nat says.

-What do you mean?

-I don't think she meant for you to show me that. I think that was like something you'd pick up at a pharmacy. Like a prescription. Or an ointment. Or a painkiller, maybe.

-It's hard when no one communicates about this type of thing.

-Do you want to try some guided meditation? Nat offers. Some hypnosis?

-I've never tried.

-Either of them?

-Either. I think it's a bad idea for me to be too close to the insides of my own head.

-Don't worry, Nat says. I'm experienced.

He pulls a chair out from the table and turns it around so that the back is facing me. He rummages in the cabinets and turns on the electric kettle. I watch as he scoops out different powders into a tin cup.

-It's tea, he says. But you can pretend it's anything.

-I think I'll pretend it's tea.

Nat gives me a small nod. The water in the kettle starts to boil. It rattles against the metal siding, trying to escape. When mist begins to leave the kettle's throat, Nat dumps it into the cup and slides the cup across the table. He then sits straddling the chair with his arms folded over the back, staring at me. I pick up the cup and blow on the surface. I think of the waves. I think of a tiny rat caught in a tiny teacup. Nat pulls out a small pendant on a silver chain and wraps the chain around his fingers. The pendant is a blue nazar eye, the kind people hang sometimes over their doorways.

-Let me know when you're finished, Nat says.

-Ok.

When the cup is empty, I can't remember how the drink

tastes. There is a numbness in my mouth only. I hear the tin make contact with the table, but I don't remember putting it there. Nat has brought the lamp over and placed it very close to his face. He is swinging the pendant now.

-Look at the pendant, Y. Follow the pendant.

-Ok.

-You are getting very sleepy.

-Mm.

-You are entering into a dream.

-Ok.

-You are abandoning all control over the waking world.

-Sure.

-And when I snap my fingers, you will be fully suspended.

-Mm.

-Elu on valu. Elu on valu. Elu...on...valu.

The pendant continues to swing. Nat raises his opposite hand and places his middle finger against his thumb as if to snap. I am in another room now.

A circular room like the lighthouse, but the walls are shaped more like a tetradecagon. The curvature has been bent. There are doors in the rooms and the doors all have heavy locks on them. The floor is made from a thick, yellow, papery pulp. I look down at the soles of my feet and see they're stained with ink. I am still wearing Nat's robe, but it seems now like it's made of iron. It feels like I'm beginning to submerge.

I look down to see faces emerging from the pulp. The faces are familiar. They are the same faces I see when I'm sleeping. There are at least three of them. It took me at least three times to realize what was happening before I stopped. I don't know where they're from. Caracas, maybe. Mogadishu. Phenom Penh. Mostly we just stare at one another. I'm not sure this is what they imagined heaven or hell to be like. I'm not sure where they go in the daylight, but I hope it's somewhere nice. I'm sure they resent the hours of the day they have to spend staring at me, but who knows what hours mean to dead people.

When the pulp reaches my kneecaps, I decide it's time to take a step. I step through the sludge in the direction of one of the doors. I can't tell whether the locks are my life or the doors are my life. I don't know which is better because neither seem to be going anywhere. I can tell now there are at least fourteen discrete doors as well, but I don't know if that number is supposed to mean anything. Only maybe three or four of them don't have locks on them. I make in the direction of an unlocked door.

-Yeah that's good. Try that one, a submerged skull says.

-You'll be back here, says another.

-Isn't it better to keep a few unlocked doors just in case you sink any further?

Typically, the voices speak Khmer, Mai-Mai, or Wayúu, but now they are speaking to me in a language I can understand. I wonder if when I talk, they can understand me now, because usually in my sleep, it just comes out as compressed air.

-Look, I'm sorry, I try telling them.

-We don't forgive you.

-If it wasn't us, it would be someone else.

-It's not even about the curse anymore, Y. It's about you.

-But don't you see that I'm trying? I ask the faces. Don't you see I'm just living from day to day?

-There is a reason for the religious obsession with forgiveness, one of the skulls replies.

-There is no escaping the opprobrium. That's the big secret.

-And there is no bargaining either way.

-So what's left for me then? I ask. Jersey?

-You'd like that, wouldn't you?

-Is that where you think you'll be with El?

-You have a miraculous way of making everything about yourself.

I feel the sludge slip past my kneecap and begin swallowing

the robe. It doesn't feel like anything. There is no sense of fear either, but the vague sensation of inconvenient abandonment one gets at losing their shoe in mud. I think there might be a way to tie the tether of the robe around one of the door handles and sit down. Cut off the air to my brain. But I think I would be too embarrassed to do that. Too worried about what the faces might think.

-I think I'll try another door, I announce suddenly.

-That's what we all thought you'd say.

-Go right ahead. They're your doors.

-It won't change anything.

I take another step and feel my ankle catch in the pulp. I bend forward, my stepping knee sinking as I reach up for the knob. It seems just beyond my fingertips. I feel the ligaments along my armpit strain. The small of my back is crushed trying to hold my chest upright in the pulp. The muscles in my fingers bear down in concentration. When I was a child, I had fine motor delay. I had trouble holding small objects. It never fully went away.

-You don't know how hard this is, I cry out.

-We don't care either, the voices say.

-Maybe if the door opens, we'll be impressed.

-Maybe everyone will.

-Maybe all your problems will go away. Behind that door.

The doorknob twitches. My free hand drops into the pulp. I push up through my shoulder to put tension on the door. The room around me starts to shake like water in a kettle being boiled. Suddenly, the whole surrounding tips over and spills out in a thick sludge onto the floor of Nat's sitting room. My face makes contact with the hardwood and the strength leaves my frame. I feel my arms are tied behind my back and my legs are blindly kicking. Then everything falls out of motion.

-Are you done? Nat says beside me.

-I think?

-Christ on a cracker, Y. That went horribly.

-You're telling me.

Nat unties the tether of the bathrobe from my elbows, and I push myself up off the ground. The sitting room has been nearly demolished. The table has been tipped over and much of the liquor shelf is now shattered across the floor. There is a large, deep cut on my right palm and my face feels very bruised.

-You had a bad reaction, Nat tells me.

-I'll say.

-I've never had anyone flip out like that.

-I told you. I told you I try to keep away from my head.

-Yeah.

I pick up Dot's scroll, the dead man's note, and Peanut's bottle from off the floor. Peanut's bottle is not broken, and I wonder if that's what he meant by it being a good one. They all smell like liquor now.

-What are those? Nat asks.

-It's a bottle Peanut gave me. And a note from the man on the helicopter.

-The dead one?

-Yeah.

-What does it say?

-I don't know, he wouldn't let me open it. He said I had to wait until the right time.

-I don't think you should have a thing like that, Nat says.

-Why?

-I think you need a long rest. I think you've put too much on yourself trying to find El's people like this. It's too much in one night.

-Maybe. But there is no other way.

-Let me take the note then. At least let me take that. You can keep the scroll, but you shouldn't be shuffling around a dead man's last message.

-What are you going to do with it?

Nat stops to think. He picks himself up off the floor and

begins to straighten things. He tips the table back over and lifts the chairs back into place. He walks carefully around the broken glass and stoops to pick up the larger pieces.

-We'll throw it into the harbor, he says. I have some cork upstairs. We'll put it into the bottle and throw it into the harbor. Kill two stones that way.

-I have no objections at this point, I tell him. I'm sorry about your floor.

-Don't mention it, Nat replies. There are a lot of people who always seem to be knocking things over and then apologizing. It's a hard way to live. Sometimes I live that way.

-Right.

I follow Nat up into the room above and hand him the note and the bottle. The lights are off, and it doesn't seem like Nat wants to turn them on. The long sweep of the lighthouse lantern throws a dim white light periodically around the room. I can make out the shapes of what look like manakins stuck in plies dressed like ballerinas, but I try not to focus on them too much.

-Follow that ladder and open the door hatch. That'll take you out into the lantern room and onto the catwalk. Don't look directly at the light.

-Sure.

I follow Nat's instructions and end up back in the air again. I can smell the storm receding after the rain. The light of the beacon feels hot on my back as it passes in rotation, and I can see —— spread out on the opposite shore. I'm not sure how long I was under hypnosis. The sky is still very dark. I can hear Nat rummaging down below. I rest my elbows on the rail. He appears a moment later carrying the bottle with a cork jammed in the top.

-Your clothes are still a little damp, he says.

-That's alright.

-I keep a lot of bottles and corks here for some reason. I try to resist the nautical theme inside the lighthouse, but these things have a way of just washing up.

-That makes sense.

-You should be the one to throw it.

-Alright then.

I take the bottle from him and test the cork. The dead man's message leans against the glass side, and I swirl it around a little. I grab the neck and pull my arm back and heave the bottle forward as far as I can. The beacon passes right as I throw. I don't see where the bottle lands.

-Did it go in the water? I ask.

-I think so.

-That's good.

Nat and I stand out on the catwalk a moment longer, but my legs start to get cold. Rituals are always disappointing in ——. We walk back through the lantern room and through Nat's bedroom and back down into the sitting area. The room smells like liquor. Nat produces a mop and bucket. I'm sure he can clean up the spilt liquid, but I'm worried about the smell.

-I'm sorry again for the shelf, I say.

-It's really fine. I feel bad. I think I need to practice my pacing a little more.

-Maybe.

Nat pushes the broken pieces into the corner. There are bruises on my skin that I am just now starting to feel.

-Do you think I can call a ferry out here? I ask.

-There's a tunnel, Nat says. Running under the lighthouse. Not many people know that it's there. You can take it to get back to the City. People sleep in it, but there's a cart on a track that'll take you. It's pretty far.

-It's on the island?

-Yeah. There's a hatch outside the lighthouse door.

Nat puts the mop down and goes upstairs to get my clothes. I feel very tired all of a sudden. I sink down onto the couch and stare at the cut on my palm. Tiny rivulets of red flow down onto my wrist. The hypnosis was very disturbing, but I'm not sure it told me anything I didn't already know. Maybe Nat is right about tonight. I'm not sure where else I can go. But I think for a minute about waking up tomorrow in my hammock. I think about brushing my teeth in the shrinking bathroom, and I want my pancreas to explode. I want my insides to contract sepsis, and I want to writhe into darkness alone on Nat's floor. He comes back with my clothes.

-That curse is pretty bad, Y, he says as I'm getting dressed.

-Yeah.

-I wish I could help you more.

-You did your best. Maybe I'll see someone about the scroll.

-You should go home, Y.

-Probably.

-You should go home.

I finish getting dressed. The clothes feel vaguely damp, but it's hard to tell. Nat and I shake with opposite hands because of the cut. I climb back downstairs.

16.

The ladder dropping down into the tunnel under the lighthouse seems longer than it should be. The faint purple circle of sky at the top of the hatch recedes. There's a dim glimmer of orange emanating up from below me, and I feel like I have been climbing in the darkness for a long time now. I wonder if they used the same paint on the ladder that they used on the playground at Oak Park. That same municipal green, rubbing off now onto my palms. Into the cut. Below, there is a radio playing, chanting the names of God. It is a good sign that the hour is not yet up.

-Is someone on the ladder? a voice asks.

-Yes, I call back.

-Do you want me to call the cart?

-If you could.

A few minutes later, I step onto ground again. There is a small landing cavern that's been carved into a hovel. A greasy mattress hugs one side of the domed enclosure. There is an easel set up with a collection of ceramic paint jars scattered around it. A set of frayed paint brushes poke up like incense sticks from the center of a small quiver. A young woman wearing a yashmak over her face sits on a stool with her hands folded together between her knees.

-Did you call the cart? I ask.

-No. Not yet. I was waiting to see if you'd come all the way down.

-I'm here now.

-Yes.

The young woman stands and crosses the room, reaching out into the darkness beyond the doorway. I see her grab something but can't tell what. Then there is the distant sound of a bell ringing. The radio continues to play.

:*sadgatiḥ satkṛtiḥ sattā sadbhūtiḥ satparāyaṇaḥ*

-Do you know where they are? I ask.

-They're going from the Vishnu Sahasranama now. They're maybe in the high six-hundreds. Maybe somewhere past that.

-Has it been slower than usual?

-About the same pace.

The woman sits down on her stool again, picks up a brush and continues to paint. My hand hurts. The cut is still fresh and the paint on the ladder has stained my palms green. I look up at the hole in the ceiling and wonder for a moment what the woman does when it rains.

-You don't have a lantern, she says softly, without looking away from her painting.

-No.

-You can borrow a candle if you like. There are some beside the door.

-Thank you.

I go over to the doorframe to a wooden box of yellowed candles. The candles look like severed limbs in the dim light. Beyond the doorway, the darkness is so intense that it is painful to look at it. I can hear the distant sound of dripping. The force of the whole bay pressing down on the earth above.

-What are you painting? I ask the woman.

-You can look at it, if you'd like.

-I wanted to be polite about it.

-I appreciate that, she says.

I pick one of the candles out of the box and walk over to behind where the woman is sitting. On the canvas, there is a cutaway picture of a woman wearing a yashmak in a dim domed room, painting at an easel. The picture she is painting is of a woman wearing a yashmak in a dim domed room, painting at an easel. And so on.

-It's a *mise en abyme*, the woman says.

-I see that.

-Do you like it?

-It hurts my head.

:ekō naikaḥ savaḥ kaḥ kiṁ yattatpadamanuttamam

The woman's mouth is obscured, but her eyes seem to slightly frown. Like the pupils became heavy. The brush she is using is very fine and she is painting perhaps the third recursion of the woman in the yashmak in the room. Her fingers move the brush very slightly. There is a set of magnifying lenses attached to a piece of headgear on the shelf of her easel.

-I would have put you in this one if you had dropped down earlier, she says. Now I think it's too late.

-How many of these have you made?

-A couple hundred, the woman replies. From all different angles. They're not particularly difficult.

-What do you do with them?

-I give them to the conductor. He tries placing them in the galleries in ——.

-Oh.

The woman puts on the magnification headgear and cleans her brush. She picks up her palette and selects an even thinner brush to dip in the acrylics.

-The conductor rents the tunnel entrances out to various artists, she says. It's a very cheap way to live.

-Do you know what they paint? I ask.

-How should I know?

-Do you know what the number of entrances is?

-No. I don't know that either. I just know this.

The woman keeps painting. Her fingers seem to move faster the smaller the strokes get. Like her hand is a hummingbird. I wonder if that's how the whole painting is. If she feels uncomfortable making the long brush strokes to fill in the shades of darkness around the painting's edge. If she feels more comfortable with the tighter brushes closer in. The mastery is in the details of the recursion.

-Have you seen my work before? she asks.

-No. I don't get out to the galleries much.

-Pity.

-Do you know Tess and Bell? I ask.

-Yes, the woman says coolly. They're hacks.

:amānī mānadō mānyō lōkasvāmī trilōkadhṛt

She flicks another magnifying lens down on the headgear and cleans her brush with her mouth, spitting the spent paint onto the floor of the domed room. I knead the candle in my hands, back and forth. Down the dark doorway, I hear the bell ringing again. This time it seems to be drawing closer.

-Fuck, the woman curses.

-What is it?

-He's nearly here.

Her fingers begin to move faster, painting at breakneck speeds but hardly moving her hands at all. The brush just seems to rock back between her thumb and index finger. The head of the brush itself is no more than three or four hairs clustered together in a thin line of stiffness. Now I can hear the sound of wheels scraping against track. A kind of rheumatic squealing in the darkness. The woman curses again and spits paint from her brush.

:samāvartō nivṛttātmā durjayō duratikramaḥ

The sounds of the wheels rattling and the rhematic squealing gets louder and louder, filling in the domed room. In the distance of the darkened door, I can see the dot of a single lamp. The cart pushing itself along. The woman pulls her final brush, hardly the size of a toothpick. She vibrates her entire wrist like an epileptic and then casts the brush aside.

-Finished, she says.

-Just in time.

She stands up from the easel and dusts off her pants. She picks up the painting, stares at it for a moment at arm's length, then holds the frame out to me. When I don't respond, she shakes the painting again. Her eyes give an impatient look. I reach out my palm, and she places the painting's frame against it. She then takes a box of matches from her pants and lights one on her boot. I hold up the candle. The flaming head of the matchstick kisses the wick.

-One more thing, she says, rummaging in her pocket. I want you to give the painting to the conductor, but I want you to have this.

-That's alright.

I hear the cart stop somewhere off in the tunnel. I feel suddenly like the conductor is waiting for me. The woman retrieves a small white pad and a fine-tip pen. She begins sketching on the pad, moving her hand with the same rapid jerks that made the final recursions of the larger painting. I glance impatiently over my shoulder as candlewax begins running over my hand.

-Shit, the woman says, rummaging through her pockets again.

-What is it?

-I need a clothespin.

-Why?

-I want to pin this to you.

-I have a campaign pin, I tell her.

-That'll do.

I set the painting down against my thigh and take out the Politician's pin. The woman takes her sketch and feeds the needle through it, attaching the paper to my jacket.

-There, she says.

-Thank you.

-Now go.

-Alright.

16.

I take the candle and the painting and disappear into the blind darkness of the tunnel. I can see the dirt beneath me and the wavering light of the cart's distant lantern. The wooden scaffolding holding up the tunnel walls. I can hear the sound of my own footsteps, the dripping of water from the bay, the conductor's breathing.

-You made it, I hear him say in the darkness.

-Yes. She has a painting for you.

-Ah.

The conductor is wearing a dark gray suit with a dark blue tie. The suit is stained with dirt and sweat. The conductor's hair is slicked over his head, and his face looks oddly young but sallow. He wears a miner's light strapped across his forehead with the bulb cracked. He takes the painting and places it in an iron sheath that's been welded into the handcar.

-Thanks for this, he says.

-It's no problem.

-It won't fetch anything but it's alright to humor her.

-I think it's pretty good.

-Do you want it then? the conductor asks. I'd have to charge gallery price, but you can have it if you'd like.

-That's ok. I'm not sure it would fit my décor.

The conductor shrugs. He twists the light on his skull and casts broken shards of pale yellow down onto the cart. He reaches a hand out and pulls me onto the iron platform. He takes the candle from me and tosses it back toward the woman's room. The light goes out. I'm sure she fetches the half-used candles of people passing through and returns them to her box. There is a twin lever beside the conductor that makes the cart run. The conductor grabs the handle on the far side, as I grab the other.

-You don't have to do it if you don't want, he says.

-Will it make it easier?

-Yes, but there's a certain rhythm we need to strike.

-We can try.

The conductor presses the handle down and my side tips up like a seesaw. The cut on my hand still stings, but I'm able to move with the metal. The cart presses a little ways down the tunnel. I push the handle down in turn. The rhythm establishes itself and the squealing of the cart resumes. The walls spread around us, beside and above the conductor's straining face. The wheels shriek like banshees in the dark.

-Do you have a lot of artists down here? I ask him.

-A fair amount. Not an exact number.

-Are they very good?

-That's not the point of art.

-I suppose you're right.

-Art is about never getting over middle school, he says.

-That's one way to put it.

As the cart presses on, the lantern light and the headlamp on the conductor's face reveal enclaves cut away into the dirt. A few of the shallow caverns show signs of being lived in. There are hammock-sides nailed into crossbeams. The scattered divots of old latrines.

-Are there others down here? I ask.

-A roving bunch. You throw a roof up and you'll attract anything. You know what they say about home, right?

-No.

-It's something we somehow haven't deserved.

-Oh.

We continue to pump the cart along. I'm afraid to see anyone down here in the dark. It would be like riding a railcar through a living room. The paper sketch the woman pinned to my jacket flaps as we roll. I feel the long, muddy drips of harbor water fall in strings above my head. I wonder if it will form another city down here. The dripping of stalagmites. There are lights glowing in the distance. I hear the radio again, very faintly beneath the grinding of the wheels.

-They'll hide when they see us, don't worry, the conductor says.

-I'm sorry to disturb them.

-It's alright. There aren't so many people who use the tunnels anymore.

-Ok.

We pass through the encampment. A small cluster of dark, maroon tents housing silhouettes stares inward at the tracks. There is a sound of shuffling as people dive behind their canvas. An odd assortment of radios crackle out the muffled signals as the broadcast approaches the end of names.

:*vihāyasagatirjyōtiḥ surucirhutabhugvibhuḥ*

-Do you know where we're going? I ask the conductor.

-The center of ——. That's where this tunnel leads.

-There are other tunnels?

-I think so.

-You don't know?

-Other tunnels, other conductors, he says. Some above and some below. This is your tunnel. Why ask questions?

-I'm just trying to get home.

-You know what they say about home, right?

-Yes.

The encampment passes behind us. The broadcast of names fades away into the dark as the squeaking sound of the wheels takes over again. My arms begin to ache. The cart starts feeling heavier than it should, and I'm wondering if it might not be easier now to walk. The fabric beneath the conductor's armpits is ripped at the seams. His legs are thin, but his chest is overbuilt. I don't think I'll be able to keep up with him much longer.

-How much further? I ask.

-We're nearly halfway there.

-Do you think we could stop at some point?

-I told you that you didn't have to help.

-It would feel strange not helping.

-Have it your way.

The conductor suddenly releases the handle. I'm aware of how much he has been boosting my strokes with his up-pull. I would not have been able to have made it this far without him. He steps off the cart.

-Look at this, he says over his shoulder.

-Look at what?

He corrects the lamp on his head again and directs it toward the wall. He cups his hand over the bulb to prevent the light from scattering. I had been so focused on the straining of the metal lever that I hadn't noticed the walls change after we left the encampment. There is no longer the same circular cavern of wet dirt. The walls are lined now with smoothed black granite. The granite has been engraved like the writing of names on a war memorial. For a moment, I wonder if it is a war memorial. I can't think of which war it might have been. The writing is fine and white and wispy. Like coils of smoke pressed into the dark.

-What is it? I ask him.

-It's a novella, I think.

-Who wrote it?

-Some guy. He crawled down here with a power drill and wouldn't leave apparently. This went on for nearly a decade.

-Is it any good?

-I don't think it's ever been read. But it looks alright, I think. Sometimes I pick up a word or two here and there. If I happen to be looking as we roll past.

-Huh.

-I'm not just an art collector, you know, the conductor says. I'm also a purveyor of rare and ancient manuscripts.

-Really?

-Yes.

I reach into my pocket and pull out the scroll Dot gave me and stick it out toward the conductor.

-What's this, he asks?

-It's a rare and ancient manuscript.

-Really?

-I think so.

The conductor pulls the scroll from its silver sheath and twists his headlamp down on it. He tilts the parchment back and forth, holding it upside-down. The shards from the lamp pierce the wrinkled page as the conductor's face writhes and twists.

-I'm a purveyor, not an interpreter, he says at last.

-Oh.

-It's a crucial distinction.

-Yes.

-There's someone on the surface though, he says. At the old Annex downtown. A professor-friend of mine. You could try it with them.

-I figured there'd be someone somewhere.

-Always is, the conductor replies.

We walk back to the cart. I sit down on the edge and the conductor takes up the lever again. I feel bad not being able to help, but the pain in my hand has started to sear. The writing on the wall flies past as the conductor pumps us along. I close my eyes. I think about sleeping and feel sick. I think about sitting with Lil and feel sick. I think the only thing that might help even a little right now is crawling into the bathtub and sinking beneath the water. There is no escape for a thing like this. I imagine the harbor smashing through the walls of the cave. I imagine drowning and wonder if that's the appeal of living down here. The cart starts to accelerate.

-Hang on, the conductor shouts.

-What's happening?

-Just hang on!

The cart tips forward. We are rolling downhill. The conductor keeps pumping the lever as the wheels shriek. Sparks shoot off into the darkness as the track before us tilts and curves. We pass the dim lights of another encampment. Unsunned faces dive behind the cover of makeshift homes. The final names of God rattle around us in a smudge of sound, the chanting obscured, ringing through the leaving halls of the cavern.

:*uttāraṇō duṣkṛtihā puṇyō duḥsvapnanāśanaḥ*

I'm knocked sideways as we careen around another curve. The conductor grabs me by the collar and pins me down against the flatbed of the cart. He releases the pump lever and seizes another handle jutting out from the undercarriage. He pulls the handle back, locking the wheels in place. The screams of the cart become deafening, blasting through the cavern, lit blue with a bushel of sparks. The cart slows to a stop.

-The way back is always a little quicker, the conductor says.

-I see that now.

Vomit spills out of my mouth. There is a door of dim light in the distance. Another artist's dome.

:*Om Tat Sat, Om Tat Sat, Om Tat Sat, Om...*

17.

The porthole to the surface slides open. I crawl out of the tunnels into someone's back driveway. The night above is wet and muggy, with the squall having washed clean over downtown ——. There are patches of scorched grass and cradles of chickweed forming cages around discarded lawn ornaments. I can see now the house here fell prey to a fire. The scorched hull of the structure bites into the night sky like rotten teeth. Crossbeams and wood siding that were corroded away by flames. I walk out of the backyard and down toward the street.

On the sidewalk, I can see where the fire started. The front of the house spreads inward like a vacant crater. A pile of wet envelopes surrounds a dented mailbox, jammed with paper like a shower drain. This is where the mystics used to live, I think. I wonder if they knew about the tunnel. I wonder if the conductor knew their names. Rain in —— never seems to make anything cleaner. It just streaks what it touches and leaves long, coppery stains. The meteorologists check the acid content from time to time, but their reports never seem to be released. It's possible the City prefers it this way.

The Annex isn't far from the old mystic house. A couple of blocks. It's where the political groups hold their meetings. When Lil was still involved with all that, I'd go down there and drink the free coffee and sit on the folding chairs and tell people my name. Lil used to be very into politics. When she felt better for a little while, she'd tell me I should get more involved with things, and I'd tell her ok. I always felt I was at the wrong meeting somehow. That the meeting just before or the meeting right after was the one I really wanted to attend.

This side of downtown is quiet. It's where the historical societies live. There are a lot of clubs in —— for studying different sides of the City, all housed in looming Victorian mansions on the west end. There are clubs for different half-decades and clubs for different defunct professions that collect obscure artifacts and have multisyllabic names. The Local Federation of Door-Collie Boot Scrapers. The Society for the Diligent Preservation of Resurrectionists and Anatomy Men. It is said by some that these societies house secret fraternal and sororal orders that conduct odd rituals late at night. It is known by most that these rituals are excuses for collecting different skin brandings, patches, and effluviums. That is what most rituals entail. A huddle of robed figures walk past me on the sidewalk, leading a goat by a leash.

-Funny weather we're having, one of them says politely.

-Always seems to be.

They shuffle on. In the distance, I can see the very peak of ——'s tall buildings above the scattered street trees. Pin Oak and Sweetgum. The clouds are low in the sky. I turn another corner and see the entrance to the Annex. There are clumps of different political associations waiting to use the space. They band together in patches on the sidewalk and whisper inwardly to one another. It's hard to say whether or not the conductor's professor-friend will be among them. It seems like he might be one of the proprietors of the space. These people are rarely seen and mostly exist to send emails too late.

-I'm looking for someone, I say to one of the banded groups. He's a proprietor here, I think.

-Good luck, one of them says back.

-The proprietors are impossible to get a hold of, says another.

-We've been trying for months, says a third.

I move down the line. Some of the clumps are talking to cars on the sidewalk, filled with more action committee members. Some are holding up long maps and doing rollcalls on the street corners to maximize the efficiency of the time they'll have inside. Some of the groups have laptops or are shuffling projectors in little green wagons. Others carry ominous black duffle bags. I approach the front and see where the queue has started at the entrance to the annex. There is an IN door and an OUT door marked with neon. There is no one guarding the door, but the weight of convention leaves the doorway unoccupied. A few moments later, a bell rings, like the bell in a schoolyard. The same type of bell they use at the Gymnasium. The group nearest the front pours into the IN door. A moment later, a fresh group pours through the OUT. I follow on the heels of the IN group.

Inside, there is a large bridal staircase that spreads down to the foyer like a pair of split wings. The main meeting area is directly between the staircases. There are a few people leaned against the banisters staring down at the group entering the hall.

-Who are they? I ask one of the people beside me.

-Graduate students, she replies.

-What are they doing up there?

She doesn't answer. We enter the hall. The group makes quickly for the rows of folding chairs. There is a detritus of Styrofoam cups and disposable plates scattered on the scratchy carpeting. I try remembering what it was Lil had said from the podium. It hadn't been that long ago, but it's impossible to form memories in ——. Only a haze of defunct actions that don't bear rehashing anymore.

-Are you from the last group? I hear someone ask.

-Get that guy's name, says another.

I realize the IN group has all turned to face me now. I'd let my mind walk away with itself. Two of them are very close and one of them seizes my jacket. They stare together down at the Politician's pin and the sketch of the *mise en abyme* pinned to my chest.

-He's a damned Syndicalist, one of them shouts.

-Get him the hell out of here!

-I'm just looking for the proprietors, I try saying but my tongue won't let me speak.

It's too late. Their hands move in concert, lifting my body like it's something they've done before. A pair of hands grabs each heel and each shoulder blade. I think absently of the Hecatoncheire as I'm tossed out of the hall. I land flat on my back beneath the bend of the staircases and feel the breath exit my body. Only the nauseous crater left in the gut when the wind is gone. My neck snaps back and my skull knocks sharply against the marble. The pain is sudden. I lay there for a while, staring up at the domed ceiling of the Annex. I don't blame them for throwing me out. What good is belonging if anyone can do it? I let my eyes slip closed and fold my hands over my stomach, staring at the darkness beneath my eyelids until a circle of heads clutter into view.

-Why'd you try that? one head asks.

-Didn't you know that was a closed group?

They lift me onto my feet. A small coterie of the graduate students came down off the banisters. The rest watch like harbor birds. I feel concussed, but I'm not quite certain. My hand still hurts something awful from before.

-I'm looking for one of the proprietors, I tell them.

-Which one?

-He's an expert in the translation of rare manuscripts.

-That could mean a couple.

The graduate students stare at me with vacant eyes. They all seem either shorter or taller than they should be. Their clothes are drab and their hair is disheveled. Like a cluster of mushroom stalks overgrown beneath a sink.

-Which one would you recommend then? I ask.

-Depends, one of the stalks says.

-You'll get a different reading for each one you pick.

-They have vastly disparate ontological groundings.

-Do you know where they are? I press.

The stalks look at one another. There are only three of them still remaining. The rest have returned to the banisters to stand with the other stalks. The remaining stalks in the foyer gaze back at the stalks on the staircase anxiously.

-They don't like to be disturbed, one stalk says.

-And they don't do translations on commission.

-So if you have money, it won't do you any good.

-I don't have money, I tell them. One of the proprietors is a friend of the conductor's. I got the manuscript on a scroll from a doctor. I'm just trying to figure out what it's for.

One of the stalks sighs and returns to the staircase. The remaining two look sympathetic, but unassured. I pull out the scroll canister from my pocket and try handing it to them. They both take a sudden step back.

-That hasn't been treated yet, one stalk says.

-We don't have that kind of training.

-I'm just looking for some help, ok? I tell them.

-Perhaps read Saussure.

Another stalk returns to the staircase. I can see the cut on my hand is green and infected. The metal case for the scroll rests above the blooming flesh as I stretch it toward the last remaining stalk.

-I'll take you to the offices, says the last remaining stalk. But you can't knock while I'm still there.

-Sure.

The stalk shuffles toward the banisters, and I follow close behind. The stalks by the banister spread as we push past them. The leading stalk puts her head down and presses through. Her face is gaunt and scarred and she walks with long, protracted steps. The staircases give way to a narrow hall where old doors face one another like they're about to dual. We reach the middle of the hallway and she pauses.

-That one, that one, that one, or that one, she says.

-Will all of them do?

-Yes, but they'll hear you if you knock on one of the other doors first, and they'll be offended. So if the first door doesn't answer, you might as well just leave.

-Do you have any suggestions?

-I could lose my fellowship for what I've said thus far, the stalk says darkly. You ask a lot, you know.

She disappears down the hallway as I confront the doors. I wonder what the dimensions of the rooms are inside. I try to imagine how the offices might stretch over the Annex Hall below, even with the hallway being so narrow. I wonder what the IN group is discussing down below. I wonder what a Syndicalist might be. I suppose it doesn't matter. I turn to the door I'm standing nearest to and knock.

A few moments later, a man in disheveled academic robes comes to the door. His gray hair pokes out like frayed wiring beneath a cap with one side dented in. His eyes are milky and hollow. His beard is untrimmed. He's eating a pear that seems to be overripe. The juices squirt out and run down his chin.

-What can I do you for? he asks.

-I need a translation.

-Alright. Come on in.

He steps away from the door, and I walk inside. The office is really two offices connected to one another, a front office and a rear one. The front office contains a large metal secretarial desk and is lined with bookshelves. There is a woman in the back office practicing violin without a bow. She plucks a few notes and then sighs.

-That's my wife, the man says. We don't talk anymore.

-Oh.

-She's a professor. Or used to be. Hard to say in these times.

-The conductor said he had a professor-friend on the surface.

-He probably meant her. I just wear the robes and tell the graduate students to go away.

-Why's that?

-They're annoying.

-Huh.

The man in the robes sits back in his chair and crosses his legs up on the iron desk. He picks up a Chinese finger trap from a cabinet drawer and sticks a thumb in either end. He pulls the trap lightly and licks his lips. I see his wife craning her neck through the doorway. She wears large glasses and cuffs the scroll of the violin.

-You're not one of them, are you? he asks.

-No.

-I didn't think so. You don't have the look.

-What are they all doing out there?

-Trying to get someone to read their theses. They wait on the staircase in case one of us has to go out to get groceries or something. Then they thrust their papers in our face.

-Why do they do this?

-They think it's the only way, the man says. It's not so bad, I just worry about what happens if they end up in one of these offices. That's how it all goes to shit. They'll believe the way they got there is the only way. They'll expect others to suffer also. Out on the staircase.

-Why not just read the papers? I ask.

-Who's got the time?

His wife is in the doorway now. Her eyes keep flitting down to my hand where the scroll is still partially outstretched. Her arms are wrapped so tightly around the violin that it's almost worrying. The fibers of the finger trap continue to contract and extend.

-She was on the Radio Drama Story Hour recap once, the man in the robes says.

-Yeah?

-You bet. Sometimes she won't shut up about it. If she's trying to impress someone. Brings it up in every other conversation if she gets the chance. They give you a certificate if you make it onto one of the panels. It's the end-all-be-all in a lot of these academic circles. The Radio Drama Story Hour. Doesn't really matter what they say as long as they've said it.

-A lot of things are like that.

-Huh. You're telling me.

The frame of the violin seems to be squeaking with the tightness of the professor's arms. She seems to be strangling the neck just beneath the scroll. I am afraid the bridge will collapse if she keeps squeezing.

-Just ask the boy for it, the man in the robes says absently.

-Ignore him, the woman sharply spits. Follow me into my office.

I cross over the floor and through the threshold. The rear office is small and warmly lit. There's a large green couch in one corner, the kind that might be found in a psychiatrist's studio. Strings of Tibetan prayer flags stretch above the woman's desk like damp washcloths on a thin clothesline on a windless day. I hand her the scroll. She unravels it and scrutinizes the vellum, hurrying the violin back into its felt case.

-Its Samogitian but it's written in cipher, she says at last, handing back the scroll.

-What does that mean?

-It's an obscure Eastern Baltic Language from Western Lithuania but it's not written outright. There's a kind of code attached.

-Anything else?

-Yes. Some illustrations. There's an etching of an ouroboros and some additional yonic inscriptions. Some further ruins I can't identify that might just be pen scratches. That sort of thing.

-Oh.

-I think it could be feasibly translated, but something tells me it's a ritual that needs to be performed. You would need to find a druid, maybe. Do you know anyone from Lithuania-town?

-No.

-I have some contacts over there, the professor says, reaching for her rolodex.

-No, no, I mutter. That's alright.

-Really, I don't mind. It might be interesting.

-It won't be.

The professor pulls away from her desk. Her eyes are magnified and distorted by the frames of her glasses and there are blotches of dry skin covering the lower half of her face. She has long, box-braided hair that sweeps over her shoulder. She wears a wool sweater with its sleeves frayed. My hand has started burning and my head aches. My ears are ringing in prolong shrieks.

-I have to go, I hear my voice say.

-Are you sure?

-Yes.

I bang into the desk in the outer office. The man in the robe jumps with his thumbs still stuck in the trap. I reach for the doorknob and throw my weight against it, struggling to press it open. I feel suddenly alone in this place. I feel suddenly like the ground is sinking beneath me. Like the room is being eaten away. Like there is a fire in the back of my skull and my optic nerves are dynamite wicks reaching out for the flame. I am afraid the door won't open and the ground will start to sink. I claw at the wood and twist the handle again.

-What's his problem, Jan? I hear the man ask his wife.

-This is not an excuse for you to say my name, she says.

The door swings open.

18.

After escaping the Annex, I find myself in the middle of the street. I'm staring into a cream-colored diner where the action groups go after their meetings. Where they drink red coffee and cold black tea. Cars swim around my shoulders on the thoroughfare. Delivery vans and taxis and dented ice cream trucks. I think my feet might be straddling the median, but I can't be quite sure. I walk further into traffic, but nothing happens to me. I walk along beside the glass panes of the diners and the coffee shops and stare at the people inside. I see my face in the reflection and the sloughs of fabric dripping off my frame. Bones like coat hangers in the back of the closet. How did I get this way? I think. Who did this to me? There are a lot of people in —— who stand in traffic, who stare at themselves in the glass facades of buildings and think up awful things. Businesses make their windows extra reflective for this exact purpose. There is a City ordinance to regulate reflectivity. Municipal employees who ensure the glass storefronts are well polished and able to show everything.

-It's that Syndicalist, someone hisses, moving past.

-I hear he tried to storm the Situationist meeting tonight.

-I thought it was a meeting for the Nation of Ulysses?

They walk away. There are a lot of reasons to never go downtown in ——. There are a lot of reasons to never go anywhere at all. I think maybe I should take the Politician's pin off but it's high on my left collarbone and my right hand hurts too much to move. Maybe I could take off my whole jacket but what if it starts to rain again? What will I do?

There's a tramline in the distance at the next intersection. The cable cars pass like green ghosts beneath the freeway on their paths to somewhere else. One of those other somewheres I know is Lithuania-town. I could go there. I could get on the ghost trams and ride in the darkness down to the Southwest side of ——. Into the hulls of the old rookeries, the old walled city, the dusty slums. There I could probably ask after a druid, ask the people on the stoops and corners of garden floors and maisonettes and benefit houses. There's a lot of goings-on over on the Southwest side. A lot of history. Names I could call after. Mel and Tip live over there, I think. Ask about El. Ask about Lil. Hear about the ones they knew who went over Jersey. I could do all of these things. Again and again.

There is a sense of foreboding in my feet now. The way you forget sometimes that you are walking. Like that walking can become like breathing or like making your heart beat. And you wonder also if there aren't a whole lot of acts like this that can fall also into weary patterns. Like maybe everything. The way that everything can become. How everything can become like patterns and suddenly, who are these faces that recur in my dreams? How did I get into this skin? Who are these people who know me and how do I know them? You are walking to a tramcar in the direction of Lithuania-town with an ancient vellum scroll full of useless, cyphered incantations. You are halfway over Jersey as it is.

Instead of walking to the tramline, I turn the corner. There is a liquor store up the street. Lil had said if I was coming back tonight, I should bring wine. It seems now that I'm coming back. The light from the liquor store falls out onto the sidewalk like a spilled glass of yellow paint. A bell rings as I push through the door. The clerk stares back sleepily though the tall glass plates. She's young, with different pieces of metal stuck in the fleshy parts of her face. The hair on her head is thick and curly. She wears a lot of plastic rings that constrict tightly around her large fingers.

The bottles in the store are all out of order. There is gin in the rye section. Vodka where the merlot should be. The statement here is obvious, and not uncommon in ——. Retailers can be expected to indulge in a certain amount of interpretive commentary. Preference is the exercise of healthy minds, I think, and in some ways, this is how all liquor stores should be. At least around here.

-Can I help you find anything? the clerk asks.

-Anything?

-Within reason.

-Ok.

I keep wandering through the sections. Soju surrounded by chianti. Mezcal alongside vermouth. There was a ballot petition a little while back to allow liquor stores to open pharmacies. I remember fleets of faces with clipboards outside of the grocery stores. I think I signed a couple of forms, but it all seems far away. This is how a lot of the ballot initiatives enter the voting booth. The election board sifts through pages of petitions with doubled-up signatures, showing support either way. Most people use their votes to spell out messages on the ballots in Morse Code.

-- / .. ... / .- / -... .-.. .- -. -.- / -.-. .. - -.--

The initiative must have passed because the clerk is wearing a lab coat over a black sweater. Either that or they hired her in expectation and now she just hangs around. There is a room in the back of the store where prescriptions might be filled, but I'm not sure that's what they use it for now. She comes out from behind the glass plating.

-Just tell me, she says. This will be a lot simpler that way.

-I don't know, I tell her. I don't drink.

-Religious or spiritual?

-It just makes me feel sad for a few days after. That's all.

-I see.

She runs her hands over some of the bottles and knocks their necks with the fake jewels of her plastic rings. She tilts the label over. Some of them are in Swedish. Some of them are in Tagalog. She places two fingers on her temples and looks sideways at me.

Like she is trying to divinate something.

-How do you feel about Muscatel? she asks.

-I've never eaten Muscatel grapes.

-But you don't have a principle against them?

-No, why would I?

-A lot of people do. This is for a friend?

-Yes.

-Close one?

-As close as one gets.

-Mm.

She picks up one of the purple bottles and clinks it against the other ones. She holds it up to the light. I think of Peanut's bottle for a moment. And the dead man's message inside. I think of it floating in the harbor around Nat's island. Or carried in with the tides to the bay. I think of someone finding it and reading the message and being bumped off in the direction of something complicated and awful. I'm glad Nat made me throw it away.

-Our bottle guy is shit, the clerk says.

-Do you know Peanut?

-Yeah. That's our bottle guy.

-Oh.

The clerk sighs and tilts the bottle upside-down. A pocket of air rises up to the surface. The weight of the wine presses down on the cork. She swirls the pocket around in a circle.

-This one is as good as any, she says.

-I'll take it then.

We walk back to the cash register, and I realize suddenly that I don't have any money. All of the cash I had I spent at the Gymnasium door. The clerk bangs out numbers on the register, and I feel guilty.

-Do you do delivery here? I ask.

-Sometimes, the clerk says. It depends.

-I just realized I don't have any money. But I might have

some back where I live.

-Huh, the clerk rubs her chin. Do you have anything to trade with?

-I have a mystic scroll written in cyphered Samogitian.

-Well that's no good. I don't know what I'd need that for.

-You could take it over to Lithuania-town and find a druid, maybe.

-That's where I live.

-Well.

The clerk rests her palms on the counter and stares up at the ceiling. I think about offering her the *mise en abyme* and the Politician's pin, but the sketch is wet and smudged and I don't think she'd want the pin.

-Where do you live? she asks.

-Oak Park.

-Huh. That's not so far away from here. It's not a bad plan.

-I'd need a ride over, I tell her. If that'd be ok.

-I figured.

She pulls a white motorcycle helmet out from beneath the counter. The detailing is chipped and the interior padding is peeling and frayed. She comes back around the plexiglass and I follow her out of the store. She stops and flips the bright *Welcome, Come On In!* sign over to display a clock with a sad face reading *Sorry, We're Closed!* There's a panel on the door where she turns off the lights. Out on the sidewalk, she locks the store with a massive padlock and pockets the key.

-It's close enough to closing time anyway, she says. This can be the one last thing.

-Thank you, I say. I appreciate it.

We walk a little further down the sidewalk. There's a dark green motorcycle with an attached sidecar parked beneath a large ginkgo tree. The sidewalk and the curb are littered with shriveled little fruits like organs in the darkness.

-I hope you don't mind the smell, the clerk says. It's just that nobody ever parks here.

-It's ok.

-The seeds are medicinal, you know? My grandmother drank them in a tea when she was going through menopause.

-I thought they carried cyanide.

-No, that's apricots. Though they look similar, don't you think?

-Yeah.

-I know someone who went over that way. With apricots.

-Mm.

-They took out sixty seeds, ground them up, and then baked them into a birthday cake. Red velvet or something like that.

-What was their name?

The clerk stares at me for a moment. She crosses her arms uncomfortably and glances up at the yellow leaves of the ginkgo tree. Some of the studs in her face catch a glare from the streetlights. The tiny silver nobs sticking out of her skin like the flecks of mica and silicon carbide embedded in sidewalks. Maybe they are meant to hold up her face.

-May. May was her name. May did that. She used to ride in that sidecar, actually.

-I'm sorry, I tell her. It's never easy.

-Do you know anyone who's gone?

-Yes. A few. I was out looking for one tonight. Or looking for his people. His name is El. Or El was his name. I'm not sure what the tenses are for that kind of thing.

-Depends on what you believe in.

-Yes.

-I'm Latvian Orthodox, the clerk says quickly, like a matter of correction. I nod and scrape a crushed ginkgo seed from the underside of my shoe onto the curb.

-I don't think I'm anything, I say.

The clerk nods. We both walk over to the motorcycle. She slips the helmet over her head and straddles the seat. I think of Dot for a moment and her racing goggles and her mobility machine. The seat in the sidecar is small and narrow and I have to suck my knees up close to my chest in order to fit in all the way.

-Did you find them? the clerk says suddenly.

-Find who?

-His people.

-No, I tell her. It has been pretty crippling. I'm giving up now.

-Oh, the clerk says. Well. It was still a nice thing for you to do. To have done.

-I suppose.

She flips her visor down and slides the bottle of wine into a pocket on the side of the motorcycle. The throttle twists and the engine comes alive. We pull out into the street.

Now the downtown fades away. Oak Park is in the opposite direction from Lithuania-town, and I feel bad pulling the clerk further from home. The sidecar is creaky and raises up when the clerk makes right turns. I think she might be heavier than me. There's a certain nausea to tipping up in the air on the thinning streets. The houses around here stand alone with long fences and large yards. The two car garages of Ash Grove. Of all the places in ——, this is where I least want to be.

In my head, there is a singular room with a large window and slatted wooden shades. I can't really remember having entered this room, but I can't remember having ever left it either. All the events of my life have taken place inside of that room. It might be that I'm hiding in there, and it might be that I have nowhere else to go. It might be it was in that room where something happened or where something was done to me. Or where I did something to someone. Everything I had, I had in that room. And everything I lost, I lost also in that room. There are a lot of rooms like that for a lot of people in ———. Although they seem to be in other rooms and with other faces, they never truly leave. Nothing on the outside truly registers but is filtered through the wall and takes on the shape of the room. It might be different for other people, but there is something in Ash Grove that speaks that room to me.

-Are you alright? the clerk asks, the bike slowing down for Children at Play.

-I'm stuck in that room where there is no movement and the light's never been.

-Oh. I know that feeling. Do you want me to pull over?

-If you would.

The clerk stops the bike and I crawl out of the sidecar. I stumble forward and sit down on the lip of the storm ditch, staring into one of the Ash Grove homes. The clerk sidles off her motorbike and tucks her helmet under her arm. She sits down beside me. The ground is wet and cold.

The house we're staring into still has its lights on. We can see into a well-furnished living room through a pair of bay windows opening out toward the street. There is a large red table beyond the walls meant for eating with the chairs around it spread far apart. A candelabra sits at the center of the table with candles that have never been lit. There are paintings on the walls of grotesque faces with their lips on the sides of their cheeks.

-Did you grow up in a place like this? the clerk asks.

-Grow is a funny word.

-I know what you mean. I have a room like that in my head

too, but it's much smaller.

-I supposed that's the unluckier thing.

-So they say. It's a certain inequivalency.

-They say if you focus on the inequivalence, you'll feel better.

-Sure, says the clerk. If you focus on the right direction of inequivalency. Gratitude being your experience in the direction of those who had it worse. Bitterness being your experience in the direction of those who had it better. So it seems.

-Those who had it worse, had it much worse.

-If you say that five times fast, you're a good person.

-I know.

The clerk picks at a patch of clover. I can hear the scrapings of her rings as they rub against one another in the dirt. There is another light on in a room of the house on the second story. The room is covered by slatted shades, but a soft yellow light still leaks out into the darkness. There are no fire escapes on the homes in Ash Grove. Even in the houses furthest up off the ground, the houses on hills. Even for the bodies that are half the size of normal height. For the bodies that would have the most to lose by jumping. That is what I hate most about coming to this part of ——.

-You should really get that hand looked at, the clerk says. It looks like it's infected.

-I think it's just paint.

-Still. That cut looks pretty deep. If I'd seen it back at the shop, I could have poured something on it. We have Spirytus Rektyfikowany in the stockroom sometimes.

-What's that?

-It's a type of highly distilled Polish liquor. We import it from Kaliningrad.

-What's it translate to?

-Rectified spirit.

-Huh.

My hand hurts something awful, but I'm not sure pouring

liquor on it would have helped. I'm not sure sitting on the roadside is helping either. It is time to leave behind Ash Grove. I stand up and reach my good hand down to help the clerk. She stands up also. We go back to the motorbike and speed off again into the night.

19.

Oak Park shoots up. The same cluster of tenement hulls, the duck pond, the abandoned jungle gym. The clerk pulls her bike right up through the courtyard where Ms Tupelo is standing over by the awning, smoking by the door. I climb out of the sidecar.

-Thank you for driving me over here, I tell the clerk. If you can wait for a second, I can find some money upstairs.

-That's alright, the clerk says. You don't have to pay for it. It was a nice drive.

-That's very kind of you.

-Sure.

She pulls the wine out of the motorcycle and hands it to me. I cradle it in my arm. I somehow lost both the *mise en abyme* and the campaign pin during the drive. Neither was particularly well attached anyway.

-I could come upstairs with you if you'd like, the clerk says. I have hypoesthesia in my vulva and lower abdomen from pudendal neuralgia so I couldn't feel anything good, but it might still be alright.

-That's ok, I tell her. I have a curse on me where every time I come, someone somewhere in the world dies. Then they haunt my bedroom when I'm sleeping.

-Oh wow, how did you get that one?

-I couldn't help someone I cared about. I think a lot of other things also had to go wrong.

-Yeah. You hear about that happening. I'm sorry, that's a tough draw.

-Yes. Thank you for the wine and the drive though.

-No problem at all.

The clerk slips her helmet back on and gets back onto her bike. She waves once and then twists the throttle, rolling out through the courtyard and back into ——. I turn toward the door to Oak Park. Ms Tupelo flicks ash from her cigarette.

-Sad day today, she tells me.

-Mm.

The coughing starts up again. Blood flicks over the pavement. I disappear beneath the rows of fire escapes and call the elevator down. Mr Kim is in the corner of the car, tweezing his nostril hairs using a dental mirror.

-How are you today, Mr Kim?

-Hrmph.

The car ascends in the direction of Lil's floor. Tiny, wiry hairs fall from Mr Kim's face. He grimaces each time he pulls the tweezers out. Teardrops gather in the corner of his eyes and he uses his bathrobe to brush them away. The car stops at (7).

-Goodnight, Mr Kim.

-Hrmph.

The hallway on Lil's floor looks much the same. The same chipped blue doors with rotting silver numbers and rotting silver eyelets. I find the one she lives behind and knock. Then step away.

-Who is it? Lil calls after a while.

-It's me, I say.

The door springs open. Lil stands behind it, wearing a satin wrap blouse with wide-legged pants and a navy blazer. Her hair is fully dark now and clipped closer to her head. The bleach is all grown out.

-Y...she says in disbelief. Where have you been?

-I was out looking for El, I tell her. I couldn't find him. I couldn't even find his friends. I brought you back some wine though.

Lil steps away from the door, and I walk past her into the apartment. Inside, all of Lil's things have been packed away. The iron-cloth sofa and the drums are gone. The posters have all been stripped off the walls. The space looks much larger than it used to, surrounded by the emptiness of long unburdened floorboards.

-Are you moving out? I ask her.

-Yes, she says. I'm nearly gone. I got a job out of town and an apartment with a yard there.

-Oh. That sounds nice.

-I think it will be.

I put the bottle down on the floor and slide off my coat. It looks worn and ragged on the floorboards now. The pin tore off a patch below the collarbone and the original color is faded from drying out and being wet again. I walk over toward the living room window and stare out of it. One of the other Oak Park tenements obscures the darkness and blocks the view.

-Is there someone else? I ask.

-No, Lil says. No one else. No more someone-elses for now. Just me.

I nod and turn to look at Lil. She's staring at me nervously. She's playing with her hands and snapping them between one another. There's a look on her face like she's just been informed the room has been pumped with radon.

-You were gone for a very long time, Y, she says.

-It's still Tuesday, right?

-You were gone for months.

-Oh.

I start feeling nauseous again. The room starts tilting and I feel suddenly very tired. There's pain in my palm that shoots up my arm and out through my shoulder blades. My body lowers itself onto the floor.

-I think you held me back, Y, Lil says. There were things I didn't process when I was with you. People I didn't become.

-That's too bad.

-I'm leaving now.

-Good for you.

I sit down on Lil's floor and listen to her footsteps as they cross over to where I'm sitting. Lil bends down next me, and I can feel her breath. She smells different. She smells like perfume.

-I saw a lot of people tonight, I tell her. I saw Ng and Tess and Bell and Zed and Dot and Nat. I saw a few other people too. None of them knew El.

-Oh Y, she says, wrapping her arms around my head. It'll be alright.

-I went everywhere.

-It'll be ok.

Lil strokes my hair. I feel her breathing on my face. Everything inside of me hurts, and I feel impossibly tired. Her body feels very far away.

-Oh Christ, Lil says, what happened to your palm?

-I cut it at the lighthouse. I think it got infected with municipal paint.

-You really need to get that looked at.

-Yeah, I say. Do you still want the wine?

-I'm sorry, Lil says. I don't drink anymore.

-Oh. That's ok.

I pull myself up to my feet. Lil steps back again. She's got makeup on and some of it is pressed onto the top of my sleeve. I see her glance at the front door. I see the long empty hallway that leads to her empty bedroom. Lil is really leaving ——.

-I'm sorry, Y, she says. I'm supposed to catch a plane tonight. I didn't know you were coming.

-That's alright. I'm sorry I came by so late.

-I really should get going.

-Mm.

We stare at each other a moment longer. We stare at all the things we did and never did. We stare at the space between us in the large and empty room. I have had a few goodbyes like this before, I think. For people leaving ——. Usually they left me with furniture or something solid. Maybe I'll empty out the bottle of Muscat and fill it with Foxglove. Belladonna or

Nightshade. That would be as good a shrine as any.

-Take care of yourself, Y, Lil tells me. Set goals and live in the moment. Eat healthy and get enough sleep. Make a list of things you're grateful for daily. Exercise and find a hobby and establish a routine. Take on responsibilities. Know that today isn't tomorrow and give yourself a break. Stay away from generalizations. Try volunteering and try to be around trees.

-Isn't there an easier way? I ask her.

-Not really, Lil says. At least there wasn't for me.

-Oh.

There's another pause. Lil looks again at the doorway. I stoop and pick up the wine bottle and tuck it under my arm. I pick up my coat too and sling it over my shoulder.

-Can I use your fire escape? I ask. I don't really want to use the elevator again.

-Sure, Lil nods. That's ok.

I walk over to her window and pull it open. The night air fills the space. I lift one leg out and then the other. Lil doesn't follow me over. She stays in the center of the room. I shut the window again and give her a small wave. She waves back. I make my way up the ladder.

I feel bad crawling past the windows between the 7th and

14th floors, but given the circumstances, I think it's ok. I try not to look inside at the people. Most of the windows are covered with pulled shades, but there are a few that stay open. The usual lonely fathers. The usual wounded face. One of the greatest perks to living in —— is that nothing ever seems to change. The clouds are the same clouds. The rain is the same rain. For as many reasons as there are to leave a place like this, there are just as many reasons to stay. —— is dependable. There are few surprises in ——. Who knows, for Lil. She may come home one day from her new life in her new city and find that a set of neon drums has sprouted in the corner of her new place. She may find that her yard has rotted away and been supplanted by an empty duck pond and a tower of interlocking fire escapes. It may happen slowly even, over a series of weeks. The buildings in her neighborhood plucked out one by one as Oak Park fills in the space. The chances of going over Jersey double the more often someone returns or the longer one stays in ——. But that's ok. There are a lot of people who have lived here before and who have made it all the way out and who have stayed away. We try not to send too many postcards.

On the 14th floor, I stop outside of my own window. The lights are still on inside and my place is still my place. My hammock still hangs in the corner. My road signs still litter the floor. Behind me, I can see most of the City out in the distance. I can see the Gymnasium and Elm Circle and the lights blinking off St Killian's North. I know in what direction the harbor lies and the lighthouse and the Annex, Spruce Flats, Lithuania-town and Ash Grove. I know this place. I tell myself and other people I've lived in —— for six months, but I was born here, I think. Or I moved here when I was too young to know what not living here means. That must be it.

Now I pull open my window.

It feels nice being home.

20.

Inside, I make my way to the bathroom. I drop my coat on the floor beside the toilet and turn on my flashlight radio. There is a long bumper on WQQX. Or else the programming is the hour for listening to different types of vinyl crackle. It could be. I shed my clothes. I twist off the cap on the bottle of Muscat and pour the wine down the sink. I pick up the vellum scroll from the pocket of my coat and stare at it for a moment in the dim light. Then I stuff it down into the bathtub drain and twist the hot handle on. The bathtub starts to fill.

In the mirror, I can see I'm just as thin as I thought I'd be. I try mentally going over the things I saw tonight, but there are gaps in my memory. The structure seems to fall apart. Or else there was someone else there, but that someone wasn't really me. I hate the things I said. I hate the things I didn't say. I hate some of the things that were said to me, but now it doesn't matter. There will be new regrets. New mistaken things. The bathtub is nearly full.

I lower myself into the water. The parchment of the scroll has swelled, clogging up the bathtub drain. I sink my hand into the water and it screams in agony. Now the paint begins to wash off. The bathwater turns an inky blue and black and green. The municipal paint mixing in with the scroll's lettering. It looks like water from the harbor. I start feeling very far away.

CULTURE, SOCIETY & POLITICS

The modern world is at an impasse. Disasters scroll across our smartphone screens and we're invited to like, follow or upvote, but critical thinking is harder and harder to find. Rather than connecting us in common struggle and debate, the internet has sped up and deepened a long-standing process of alienation and atomization. Zer0 Books wants to work against this trend. With critical theory as our jumping off point, we aim to publish books that make our readers uncomfortable. We want to move beyond received opinions.

Zer0 Books is on the left and wants to reinvent the left. We are sick of the injustice, the suffering and the stupidity that defines both our political and cultural world, and we aim to find a new foundation for a new struggle.

If this book has helped you to clarify an idea, solve a problem or extend your knowledge, you may want to check out our online content as well. Look for Zer0 Books: Advancing Conversations in the iTunes directory and for our Zer0 Books YouTube channel.

Popular videos include:

Žižek and the Double Blackmain

The Intellectual Dark Web is a Bad Sign

Can there be an Anti-SJW Left?

Answering Jordan Peterson on Marxism

Follow us on Facebook
at https://www.facebook.com/ZeroBooks and Twitter at https://
twitter.com/Zer0Books

Bestsellers from Zer0 Books include:

Give Them An Argument
Logic for the Left
Ben Burgis
Many serious leftists have learned to distrust talk of logic. This is
a serious mistake.
Paperback: 978-1-78904-210-8 ebook: 978-1-78904-211-5

Poor but Sexy
Culture Clashes in Europe East and West
Agata Pyzik
How the East stayed East and the West stayed West.
Paperback: 978-1-78099-394-2 ebook: 978-1-78099-395-9

An Anthropology of Nothing in Particular
Martin Demant Frederiksen
A journey into the social lives of meaninglessness.
Paperback: 978-1-78535-699-5 ebook: 978-1-78535-700-8

In the Dust of This Planet
Horror of Philosophy vol. 1
Eugene Thacker
In the first of a series of three books on the Horror of Philosophy,
In the Dust of This Planet offers the genre of horror as a way of
thinking about the unthinkable.
Paperback: 978-1-84694-676-9 ebook: 978-1-78099-010-1

The End of Oulipo?
An Attempt to Exhaust a Movement
Lauren Elkin, Veronica Esposito
Paperback: 978-1-78099-655-4 ebook: 978-1-78099-656-1

Capitalist Realism
Is There No Alternative?
Mark Fisher
An analysis of the ways in which capitalism has presented itself
as the only realistic political-economic system.
Paperback: 978-1-84694-317-1 ebook: 978-1-78099-734-6

Rebel Rebel
Chris O'Leary
David Bowie: every single song. Everything you want to know,
everything you didn't know.
Paperback: 978-1-78099-244-0 ebook: 978-1-78099-713-1

Kill All Normies
Angela Nagle
Online culture wars from 4chan and Tumblr to Trump.
Paperback: 978-1- 78535-543-1 ebook: 978-1-78535-544-8

Romeo and Juliet in Palestine
Teaching Under Occupation
Tom Sperlinger
Life in the West Bank, the nature of pedagogy and the role of a
university under occupation.
Paperback: 978-1-78279-637-4 ebook: 978-1-78279-636-7

Ghosts of My Life
Writings on Depression, Hauntology and Lost Futures
Mark Fisher
Paperback: 978-1-78099-226-6 ebook: 978-1-78279-624-4

Sweetening the Pill
or How We Got Hooked on Hormonal Birth Control
Holly Grigg-Spall
Has contraception liberated or oppressed women?
Sweetening the Pill breaks the silence on the dark side of hormonal
contraception.
Paperback: 978-1-78099-607-3 ebook: 978-1-78099-608-0

Why Are We The Good Guys?
Reclaiming Your Mind from the Delusions of Propaganda
David Cromwell
A provocative challenge to the standard ideology that Western
power is a benevolent force in the world.
Paperback: 978-1-78099-365-2 ebook: 978-1-78099-366-9

The Writing on the Wall
On the Decomposition of Capitalism and its Critics
Anselm Jappe, Alastair Hemmens
A new approach to the meaning of social emancipation.
Paperback: 978-1-78535-581-3 ebook: 978-1-78535-582-0

Enjoying It
Candy Crush and Capitalism
Alfie Bown
A study of enjoyment and of the enjoyment of studying. Bown
asks what enjoyment says about us and what we say about
enjoyment, and why.
Paperback: 978-1-78535-155-6 ebook: 978-1-78535-156-3

Color, Facture, Art and Design
Iona Singh
This materialist definition of fine-art develops guidelines for
architecture, design, cultural-studies and ultimately social
change.
Paperback: 978-1-78099-629-5 ebook: 978-1-78099-630-1

Neglected or Misunderstood
The Radical Feminism of Shulamith Firestone
Victoria Margree
An interrogation of issues surrounding gender, biology,
sexuality, work and technology, and the ways in which our
imaginations continue to be in thrall to ideologies of maternity
and the nuclear family.
Paperback: 978-1-78535-539-4 ebook: 978-1-78535-540-0

How to Dismantle the NHS in 10 Easy Steps (Second Edition)
Youssef El-Gingihy
The story of how your NHS was sold off and why you will have
to buy private health insurance soon. A new expanded second
edition with chapters on junior doctors' strikes and government
blueprints for US-style healthcare.
Paperback: 978-1-78904-178-1 ebook: 978-1-78904-179-8

Digesting Recipes
The Art of Culinary Notation
Susannah Worth
A recipe is an instruction, the imperative tone of the expert, but
this constraint can offer its own kind of potential. A recipe need
not be a domestic trap but might instead offer escape – something
to fantasise about or aspire to.

Paperback: 978-1-78279-860-6 ebook: 978-1-78279-859-0

Most titles are published in paperback and as an ebook.
Paperbacks are available in traditional bookshops. Both print and
ebook formats are available online.
Follow us on Facebook
at https://www.facebook.com/ZeroBooks
and Twitter at https://twitter.com/Zer0Books